Praise for *Leaving Tabasco:*

"This is an edgy, funny, and sometimes frightening book about an exhilarating and awful Mexican childhood. It is also an ode to the now-vanished secret heart of southern Mexico: its vast mahogany jungles and the constricted, tradition-bound, violent, and yet enchanting small-town life that until recently thrived along the jungle's edges. Carmen Boullosa writes with a heart-stopping command of language. Her recollection of a child's emotions is implacable and unerring, her sense of history precise. A beautiful work."

—Alma Guillermoprieto, author of
The Heart that Bleeds and *Looking for History*

"Delmira Ulloa watches all these proceedings with a placid disposition and a wry sense of humor. . . . Putting into question the very dependability of our realities, this playful novel aims to muddle in order to help us better see."

—Irina Reyn, *San Francisco Chronicle Book Review*

"A lovely, aromatic mix of small-town portraiture and coming-of-age story, heavily seasoned with magical realism . . . So rich that we happily share with her the myriad components of her life, including the infinitely charming town she inhabits; her grandmother's fantastic imagination; and the mysteriously absent father 'who had been eliminated by the women in [her] home.'"

—Erica Da Costa, *The Washington Post Book World*

"Raucously imagined . . . a meditation on family, community and storytelling. . . . In her hard-won wisdom and courage, Delmira is . . . fascinating."   —Carlene Bauer, *Time Out New York*

"A luminous writer . . . a delightful coming-of-age tale filled with the kind of exulting magical realism that seemed to have run its course in Latin American literature."

—Fabiola Santiago, *The Herald* (Miami)

Leaving Tabasco

Leaving Tabasco

Carmen Boullosa

Translated from the Spanish by

Geoff Hargreaves

Grove Press / New York

Published simultaneously in Canada
Printed in the United States of America

Originally published as *Treinta años* in 1999 in Spanish by Alfaguara (Mexico City)

FIRST PAPERBACK EDITION

Library of Congress Cataloging-in-Publication Data
Boullosa, Carmen.
    [Treinta años. English]
    Leaving Tabasco / Carmen Boullosa ; translated from the Spanish by Geoff Hargreaves.
    p. cm.
    ISBN 0-8021-3860-8 (pbk.)
    L. Hargreaves, Geoff. II. Title.
    PQ728.12.O76 T7413 2001
    863'64—dc 21   00-063656

Design by Laura Hammond Hough

Grove Press
841 Broadway
New York, NY 10003

02 03 04 05   10 9 8 7 6 5 4 3 2 1

"Fancy is dead and drunken at its goal."—John Keats

"Stay away from the impossible, for wisdom states that we should copy only what is likely."—Lope de Vega

To Gustavo Velásquez, Yolande del Valle, Luis Ro and Ale, and to my sister María Dolores, who shared my shawl.

1997

1

The Winter of the Flu

Everything was bound to change, I realized, when I started to imagine—and couldn't stop imagining—that the virulent outbreak of flu was spreading far and wide. My imagination had hit the mark in one sense at least. The winter had lasted longer than usual and the early morning temperature was still stuck at twenty below, even in the first days of March. Anybody who hadn't already succumbed to bronchitis and a cough was scheduled to do so. But the problem wasn't just the physical misery that spared nobody; people had gotten so bad-tempered that they made the lead-gray sky look even grayer with faces that reflected the grayness. You couldn't have found a smile on any passing face, not even by mistake. As kids came out of school, they moved among the silent passengers of the U-Bahn with the sinister docility of grim miniature adults.

O Germany! who could love you in that condition? In similar years—though no winter had been quite so prolonged and so severe—I had floated through the surrounding gloom, buoyed up by the memory of my native sun. Recalling its heat filled me with an angry vigor. I was the one who walked faster on the streets, I was the one who spoke louder when I bought bread. But now my last reserves of energy had been drained away by my sickly fantasy: the whole world was coming down with flu.

The flu of my imagination was not scary and overpowering. It was the flu, nevertheless; headache, body aches, tiredness, sneezing, a nonstop dripping of the nose, shivers, phlegm, and an intermittent cough, a sly cough that made everybody sound alike, regardless of sex or physical build. This flu was, like all its other manifestations, contagious and frankly incurable. Cold medicines and antihistamine tablets couldn't make a dent in it. The only help was aspirin, and even that didn't do much. And soon we ran out of it. The pharmacies began closing down, and there was a shortage of the more important drugs. The flu was inoffensive only in appearance. Nobody who caught it could carry on working after two or three weeks; they couldn't concentrate or even think. They couldn't carry loads or make the least physical effort, not even a basic movement. Their routine collapsed, however light it might be. Everybody was falling victim, inexorably, to what you might call the appearance of laziness. This is what I was imagining in my effort to fight off the lousy German winter: that humanity was coming to an end without any grandiose, trumpeting announcements, with no fuss at all really, just sliding down into something close to an uncontrollable melancholy. Little by little the end was drawing near, like a fading light, like a slowly dying fire, till nobody would be left and the words THE END could be read upon the surface of the earth.

While I worked on the final touches of my fantasy—I was debating between mass suicides or having people curl up and die, as they tried to cough up the phlegm that was suffocating them—it suddenly struck me that my life was going to change. That winter I hadn't drugged myself with consoling dreams of the sun, because—elementary, my dear Watson—I would soon be experiencing its warming rays in person, upon my own flesh. My long stay in Europe had drawn to a close. Thirty years, Delmira, thirty years had come and gone for you.

1961

2

Introducing My Family

I was eight years old when I first saw the scene. She was midway between me and the street. I was in the inner patio of the house, perched on an edge of the fountain, mindlessly watching a parade of ants, simply killing time.

The entrance to the patio was on my right. The passageway which led to the main door of the house was closed only at nightfall. Ours was a house where only women lived, if we overlooked the son of one of the granddaughters or the great-granddaughters of the elderly Luz, who now lived with us, if you can call it living when you're lying faceup in a crib, incontinent, humming away to yourself like some aimless fly, with nobody sparing you a glance, living from one day to the next almost by a miracle. When it got dark, we shut the door tight, but the rest of the time we left it wide open, and anybody who wanted to could come in or go out without a by-your-leave, the way things were usually done in Agustini. At sunset my grandmother herself, with her black shawl over her shoulders, personally checked that the bar was placed across the door.

The shawl business was overdone, a pointless affectation. In our region the weather was extremely hot all year round. There were only two seasons, the rainy and the dry, and if it was really true that it "got chilly" at nightfall, as we used to put it, it's also true that not even December merited a black shawl, knitted by nuns in remote latitudes for a vastly different climate, because even when it "got chilly," we were still waving fans to cool ourselves down.

The shawl was the visible sign of her widow's dignity and of her withdrawal from the world. With the shawl spread over her shoulders, nobody could doubt her grandmotherly purity and seriousness. She was an old phony, but, thanks to the shawl, we were supposed to believe in her chaste antiquity. The phoniness became clear when I did a little math. I was born when my mother was sixteen. She was born when Grandma was the same age. Add on my eight years and you only get forty. She loved to whine that her feet gave her trouble, but I suspect that her continual whining was just one more affectation, like the nighttime shawl, because all day long she traipsed around, coming and going with the obstinate energy of a skinny young woman, without the least sign of pain in either foot. Her problem didn't go beyond the merely verbal. I never saw her having to lie down for any reason. When I awoke, she was already wide-awake, fully dressed, darting here and there; and when I went to bed, it was the same. The only difference was that by bedtime she had let down her long, partly white hair, so that it could get its combing, and had carefully folded her shawl and placed it like a cat on her lap. The whiteness of her hair was the sole attribute that suggested age. Yet, though it revealed its white streaks, once she had let it down, its length and thickness still had the gleam of youth.

The household followed a clockwork routine. I would curl up in my hammock, while Mama rocked in her chair in front of Grandma. My nanny, Dulce, stood behind Grandma and combed her hair with a variety of combs, starting with the biggest comb with the widest-set teeth. She worked with care, while Grandma spun her tales nonstop. If it was Lent, the tales gave way to endless rosaries, but what generally and best lulled me to sleep were the stories of adventure: of my great-grandfather in the jungle, his brother the tiger hunter, an uncle who was bullet-proof, the rebels who passed through town like an urgent cloud of dust, the statue of the Virgin that had a nest of snakes in the twelve folds of its dress, the picture of the child Jesus which spoke when a pinko general ordered its removal. She rarely repeated her stories, at least not in the same words. When she prayed, the phrases re-sounded in my ears, scaring me for a variety of reasons, incapable of soothing my fears. It was the stories, all of them involving the family, that stayed with me. They always put me to sleep. It was years before I stayed awake long enough to hear the conclusion of even one of them.

At home only my hair got brushed, as if they felt obliged to pamper me in some way. Otherwise, I was like a child who had wandered into the house by mistake, like the babies of the family of old Luz, who were dumped on us for weeks or months, except that they had abandoned me for much longer. They paid me almost no attention. And not even those tall tales, told by candlelight to keep away the flies—though it attracted moths—were intended for me. So I could do whatever I'd a fancy to, for nobody was keeping an eye on me.

The whole town knew about the presence of those aban-doned babies, left with Luz in our house. I'm not sure by what quirk of fate one of the kids turned into a tattletale in the home of the Juarez family, but they said that he still hadn't lost the stink of pee. And we all believed it was true. I had only to catch a glimpse of him to smell pee, though it wasn't unusual on a mar-ket day for a man to urinate freely against any wall whatsoever, in full view of everybody, without a second thought. So much urination went on, all around, that nobody thought anything of this shameless activity. The stink seemed an inevitable part of life. It rose up spontaneously, with or without the aid of the Juarez's tattletales.

I know for sure the smell of pee never left the bedroom of old Luz. Her room always smelled the same, whether or not it contained a squawking baby. I was strictly forbidden to enter there. Luz and my nanny, Dulce, slept there. My mother had firmly vetoed my entrance. I think it was the only order she ever gave me, and I obeyed it as far as I could. I've never displayed exemplary willpower, and so, without a word to anybody and without any fuss, I popped in now and then to check its condition. Disorder and slovenliness reigned supreme, unlike in other rooms of the house, unlike even in the cupboard under the sink, where we kept, among other things, the tops from broken jars, a fork that didn't match any set, and the hand of a grandfather clock that nobody could get to stay on the clockface. Even that seemed a model of cleanliness compared to Luz's room, where her stuff lay in slatternly confusion: a garter, a jar of cream, matches, a discarded price tag, the bedside lamp, a pencil, all higgledy-piggledy, along with a holy picture of the bleeding heart of Jesus, with Jesus himself pointing to it, pulling open his robes to reveal his own insides, like a wounded animal, skinned but miraculously alive, withstanding all the agony we sinners inflict on him.

Dulce, the nanny in charge of me, must have been around thirteen years old at that time. Now that I think about it I realize how young she was, but back then I considered her old. And I knew she was as tough as nails. She was a hard-nosed cop trained by Grandma. She had worked in the house since she was seven years old and had had only one year of schooling. In that time she learned to write numbers on a piece of paper, add, subtract, write her name and all the letters of the alphabet, and read by spelling out the syllables. That, she figured, was enough education. In the house she had learned to knead dough for tamales, and to dry and grind cocoa for the chocolate which Grandma made into little slabs, leaving her fingerprints all over them. She knew how to make a paste for almond milk by peeling the nuts in hot water and then grinding them in a mortar. In recent years they had even initiated her into the mysteries of fire. They now allowed her to stir the caramel paste in the copper saucepan and to watch the jams so that they didn't stick to the pan or over-cook. She did all this while I was at school, or if school wasn't in session, while I goofed off or buried myself in a book from Uncle Gustavo's study, because, for sure, they weren't teaching me a single damned thing. I felt like a stray kid in the house, while Dulce was their favorite grandchild. If I peeped into the kitchen, while Dulce was deboning a hen for a celebratory supper, she'd no sooner realize I was there than she'd be ordering me out with "You're gonna knock over a pot," though there wasn't a sem-blance of a pot in sight, only the meat grinder on the corner of the table or maybe the rolling pin or the scissors. "Go on, get outta here, before you burn yourself on the stove," she'd holler, though the stove was at the far side of the enormous kitchen. Or it was "You're going to get your clothes dirty," when my dress was already far dirtier than her spotless apron.

Dulce knew all the culinary secrets of my grandmother, stuff neither I nor my mother knew. She was not the cooking expert, however. That was still old Luz, who'd been top dog in the kitchen for as long as Uncle Gustavo had been alive. Now she was so old that she seemed incapable of motion. When she ar-rived at the house, her letter of recommendation said: "You can have this old woman. To look at her, you wouldn't think she was worth a penny, but she does know how to make a stew and to get shirts whiter than anybody I've met." But she was too old to beat the mixture for the meringue pie or put the heated spoon on the cream to make a caramel sauce. She couldn't even hold it over the fire to get it red-hot. She did only a certain number of

things and even today I'm surprised that a woman so slow on
her feet that a superficial glance barely detected a sign of life in
her could still do them. It was the ancient Luz, now past her
hundredth birthday, who killed the turtle, first cutting off its head
and then scooping it out of its shell, to make the black stew that
only she knew how to cook. It was she who plucked and chopped
up the ducks and chickens. She was the one who skinned the
live iguanas. Only she made buns stuffed with beans, the best
lentil soup in the world, with slices of banana and chunks of spicy
pork sausage, and the refried beans which deserved a medal. (Their
glorious condition owed much to the addition of vast quantities
of corn oil.) Only she made tortilla pockets containing crunchy
deep-fried pigskin, and meatballs flavored by a minute pinch of
caramel, and almond chicken, and fluffy flan, and flawless chops
in red wine, and cheese stuffed with two sauces of different flavors
and colors, hollowed out with the point of a knife she never let
leave the kitchen, because its edge, filed to a dangerous sharpness,
was capable of slicing off your tongue. She could hardly walk a
step, but, unlike Grandma, she never complained. She always said
she was fine, that she'd never felt better. Sitting on her wooden
chair, she spent hours working with her misshapen hands, midway between the sink and the stove, with a saucepan near her right
foot and a metal bucket with clean water at her left side. And when
she'd finished her labors, she'd clap her hands together, like a small
child, with the fingers wide apart, while she chanted songs (with
which she should have been calming the current baby, who would
inevitably be howling in her room), songs with which she greeted
my arrival in the kitchen, in a singsong all her own:

> *O where is my little Delmira?*
> *Come nearer, my darling, come nearer.*
> *I've kisses and cuddles to give you,*
> *And sugar candies to feed you.*

The song ended, there followed the obligatory distribution of caramel wrapped in shiny black paper, with a little white cow on it, announced by still other doggerel verses from this woman who shrank more and more each day. If Dulce was present, she'd confiscate my candy "till after dinner," a till-after that rarely materialized. The candies, I suspect, ended up in Dulce's own mouth.

Certainly old Luz was sitting there in her chair on the afternoon I'm talking about, but who knows what Dulce was up to, whether preparing something in the kitchen or rushing off on some errand for Grandma, while I was sitting on the rim of the fountain watching the bustle of the ants. Suddenly—I can't tell you why—I raised my eyes from the fountain and saw her. The door of her room was ajar, so there was enough space for me to inspect her. Behind her, one of the balconies that overlooked the street was half open. The sunset had painted the sky a brilliant pink. The torsos of passersby and Mama's figure were outlined with vivid sharpness. I could see not just her long, loose hair but every detail of the dress she was wearing, almost as if I could touch her, a flimsy shift of fine linen that stirred in the breeze, clinging to her body like a second skin, a body that was shaking with mild fits of laughter. She was clutching a water jug with a metallic base to her side. Drops of water dripped to the ground.

Her room was built two feet above street level and maybe this was why the breeze was lifting up her light shift, exposing her pretty calves. She was all curves, the way I am nowadays. Both of our bodies are devoid of sharp angles, without being chubby. Whoever designed us—a stumpy god, presumably, because he made us both short—had no knowledge of straight lines. Since I was perched on the rim of the fountain, we were both at the same level. People kept on passing by without stopping to look at her. She raised her shift with her left hand. The sky was now a fiery red, staining the dying day with colors of heat. Inflamed by the hues of the sky, I felt it in my own body when Mama's right hand emptied the jug over the black triangle of her crotch. She let the vessel drop and wiped the water sliding down her thighs back up to her crotch. She did it again and again. The water seemed to run down in slow motion. Mama was bending forward and then tossing her head back with the grace of a dancer. She was clinging to the balcony rail, and it didn't seem to bother her that people in the street could see her shameless performance.

My, but she was beautiful! Still, that was no excuse for her to be exposing her nakedness in this scandalous way. Occasional passersby glanced up at her from the corners of their eyes, but they went on their way without raising any hue and cry. I was the only one who was shocked.

I could see the hammock in Mama's room, a little to one side. It started to sway back and forth. But Mama hadn't changed her position. Then the door through which I could see her slammed shut in my face. An alarm went off deep in my brain: "There's somebody with her!"

I ran to find Grandma, because I didn't know what else to do, and I had to do something. The red of the sky had tinted everything. The whole world was on fire. The ants I had been watching seemed to scurry up the inside of my throat. It was the time of day for the mosquitoes, but I couldn't hear a single insect sound because everything inside me was buzzing.

I found Grandma in her bedroom, shaking up the mattress, punching it with the energy of a girl. "Grandma, Mama isn't alone," I told her. "Hurry up. They're going to do something horrible to her."

She ran behind me, still without her shawl over her shoulders, despite the rapid approach of night. She then overtook me, sweeping into Mama's room like a tornado. The window of the balcony that overlooked the street was still partway open and

Mama was stretched in her hammock, her hair down, her shift pulled halfway up, and her legs shiny with water. Her eyelids were half closed. There was nobody with her. Grandma grabbed the pole which we used to gather fruit from the trees in the garden and which Mama kept in her room like some kind of treasure, and started to whack her with it, calling her a filthy bitch, while Mama kept saying, "What's the matter, Mama? What's up with you? You're going to break the pole. It's for the mangoes. Stop it!"

But Grandma didn't stop until the pole broke and then she bellowed at her, "So you did have somebody in here!"

"What are you talking about? Who did I have in here? I've been alone all afternoon with the door shut."

"Delmira says you had somebody here."

My mother narrowed her eyes at me. "Did you see anybody? Why would you want to tell a lie like that?"

"I didn't see anybody. But I did see the hammock swinging. And somebody slammed the door."

My answer made her take her eyes off me and she glanced submissively at Grandma.

"It was the wind, Mama. I swear it. Who could I have had in here?"

Grandma now glared at me in fury. It was probably the first time in her life that she had really looked at me.

"You bitch!" she screamed with the full force of her lungs. "I should smash your head open! But I don't have the energy to waste on you. Did you hear me? You little loser! You misbegotten good-for-nothing! You, you, you . . . !" This "you" she howled out, pointing at me, drawing out the vowel, as if she wanted to blow me away. But she didn't finish the sentence. That "you" was enough to convict me of being the lowest of the low.

She leaned over Mama and covered her with kisses, begging her forgiveness. I stood there like a total fool, saying noth-

3

The Shawl Store

A few days later I went shopping with Dulce. She had three precise errands for my grandmother, who had already set out early to buy the weekly groceries. Dulce had to bring home some cinnamon, a bunch of scented cloves, and a skein of white wool for crocheting. There was no boy along with us to carry the goods. Thinking herself alone in the middle of the hubbub (apart from me, of course), she had let her mind wander. At first she was leading me by the hand, very attentively, but after a while she let go my hand and actually forgot she was in charge of me. She hardly seemed to remember what she was going for. For sure, she wouldn't notice my absence, so I quit following her through the crowds and smartly slipped away.

It was Saturday, market day, and there was lots of bustle because it was also the occasion of some Indian festival. Booths extended alongside the church and its ample porch, crowded with vendors who had come down from every part of the region and were flooding the neighboring streets with their merchandise.

I was carrying on me all my savings, the money that Uncle Gustavo slipped to me behind Grandma's back. He no longer lived with us, having moved to the city, but he came back for parties and birthdays. "In this house full of lovely ladies," he liked to say, "you, Delmira, are my favorite." I kept every coin and bill he gave me, never spending a thing, because they were my only treasure. But now I had them all with me, as I had decided to get Mama a splendid present so that we could be friends again. I was going to buy her another long pole for gathering fruit, one with a small woven basket at the top which could collect the fruit from the topmost branches without letting it fall to the ground. I was going to replace the one Grandma had broken across her shoulders, but I was going to take her something else as well, something very special, something that would never wear out, something that would be hers alone. It was a stroke of luck that Dulce had let her thoughts wander and had forgotten all about me, because it would have been far from easy to buy something really special with that tough character by my side. She modeled herself on my grandmother and would not have countenanced any extravagance.

I checked out the stalls selling various kinds of tackle and bought the longest pole I could find, much longer than the one that had gotten broken. I scanned the hats for sale with a careful eye, but I couldn't find one that struck me as really special. Then I toured the haberdasheries inside the market, but I still couldn't decide on anything. I came out through the rear entrance, where cookware was for sale, and live animals, and I nosed around there, more out of curiosity than anything else, since I'd never explored that section of the market. For a moment I thought I'd get Mama a duck or a turkey. Then I considered a small plate, hand-painted with flowers, where she could keep her hairpins and clips. I almost decided on a pair of extra-sharp, elegantly designed scissors, and I already had them in my hand when I spotted what I was looking for. Between a stall selling gigantic clay pots and dishes, so big they could have been used for elephant soups or cannibal stews, and another with copper spoons and ladles of all sizes, there on the ground, on a large white sheet, beside an unbroken line of long veils, white, gray, and black, which didn't interest me in the slightest, was a display of rebozos, shawls, hand-kerchiefs, wraps, and head scarves in different shapes and sizes, and in an endless variety of colors. Immediately I darted to the stall. I planted myself in front of it with my pole set upright be-side me. The scarf that first caught my attention was a red one, small in size but of fine texture.

"Who do you want that for, little girl?" the salesman asked me in a voice whose accent was strange to me. "That isn't much good for anybody. Better take this one."

He spread in front of me a big, beautiful head scarf, of golden yellow, almost honey-colored. He held it for a moment at the height of my waist and it seemed to settle, almost of its own volition, down my front. Then he showed me another, a long-ish one, brick-red, which floated lightly up to the top of my pole, which rose above me, along with the first scarf, both of them spreading out overhead. One after another, he laid out scarves, wraps, and shawls and let them hover in the air till we were both contained beneath an impromptu, floating tent of bright hues, whose peak was the point of my pole. The sunlight filtered in between the articles, caging us in light and subtly graded shad-ows. In the middle of the bustling Saturday market, he had made a cool tent for us, using just the breeze and the fruit-collecting pole. When he saw that we were alone in our enclosure, he said to me, "Which one do you want, Delmira? Pick out a head scarf. You don't need to pay me. It's a present. I'll give it to you free on one condition: that you don't choose a black shawl like your grandma's. And in return, I ask one thing, your silence. Don't tell anybody you've seen me or mention anything I've shown you. Because old Skin-and-Bones won't forgive me for making this tent, or her daughter either. They don't want you to see anything. They don't want you to know anything. But you're already aware of that. You are their jewel that stays put. They'd love to shut you away in their drawers, if I can use the word 'love' for their feelings toward you. They are two old misers. Their hearts are carved out of stone. The daughter will soon turn into skin and bones like your grandmother. Come on now, take one of the scarves."

I couldn't say yes or no. I didn't dare open my mouth.

"Which do you want? Pick one. It's for your mom, right?"

I nodded, staring at him. I felt I could trust him. It was true, what he'd said.

He chose for me, the beautiful brick-colored scarf, either because he was running out of patience or because he wanted to end my hesitation. As he folded it up, our tent broke apart. The magic spell of the faint, trapped light was broken. But my mind remained entranced. As soon as he put the scarf into my hands, I couldn't help myself. I kissed him on the face, murmuring my thanks. He gave me a long, tender hug, as nobody ever had before in all my life. He pulled down the shawls and scarves one by one, folding them carefully and returning them to their former places, and then he asked me for mine so that he could wrap it in sand-colored paper.

"Not a word about me at home, eh?"

"No. I promise."

"Do you remember your daddy?" he asked.

"Do you know him?"

"You need to understand that the shawl comes to you from him. I know him very well."

"Why don't you ever come to see me?"

"I'll tell you something, but you must swear to keep it a secret. Listen carefully: The man who fornicated with the grandmother would produce a child in the daughter. But if he fornicated with the daughter and made her womb fruitful, he'd have to leave home forever and ever."

"What's for-ni-cate?"

"Learn my secret message by heart. You'll understand it when you understand it."

I sat down on the edge of the stall, beside the chair that belonged to the woman selling cookware, and memorized the saying, repeating it over and over, determined I'd never forget it. I shut my eyes tight in order to concentrate better. "The man who for-ni-cated . . . ," spacing out the syllables in an effort to understand their sense. Behind my voice I could hear the hubbub of the market, the sounds of animals, a donkey, and somebody farther away calling out, "Six for the price of five!" I raised my face to the sky and opened my eyes to see clouds of oranges passing overhead. So orangey I could smell oranges.

"It'll soon rain orange blossoms," said the Indian woman at the cookware stall when she saw me following the cloud with my eyes, "and all the girls will be getting married. But don't you be one of them."

I laughed. I was eight years old. How was I going to get married?

"I'm a little girl, lady. How could anybody marry me?"

"People don't care about things like that. They married me off when I was your age."

"To your husband?" I asked, because that's all I could think of. I imagined her as a little girl on the arm of a grown man, her elderly husband, with his beard and paunch, and she, poor thing, no bigger than me.

"Of course to my husband. Who else do you suppose? But my luck wasn't all bad. He died a while back."

"Was he very old?"

"Not old at all. They killed him with a machete in a quarrel, because he was one of those who wouldn't vote for the government."

"I'm so sorry!"

"You don't have to feel sorry for me, dear. He got what he
deserved. He was a—" She fell silent, not telling me what he
was.

I got up, dusted off my skirt and smoothed it down. I
checked to see if the straps of my sandals were fastened. Then I
picked up my pole and slipped the packet with the head scarf in
it under my arm. I searched with my eyes for the man with the
shawls, veils, and rebozos. He was scribbling something on a piece
of paper, resting it on some cardboard. He stopped, as if sensing
my glance on him, and said, "So you're leaving already, are you?
What's the big hurry? Don't tell me you're longing to go back
to the lap of old Skin-and-Bones!" He smiled.

I shook my head no. It was true; I was in no hurry to go
home, but I didn't want to stay there, either. I was thirsty and I
think I was getting hungry as well.

"All the same, I'm going. I'm thirsty."

"Here!" he said, looking for a coin in his trouser pocket,
and when he pulled one out, he said, "Go buy yourself a *pepito*."

He gave me a peso. *Pepitos* were plastic bags full of frozen
water in various colors, sold at the corner of our street. They
were long and thin and you broke off the top and sucked it. The
coloring stained your mouth, green or blue, but they all tasted
alike: of water with lots of sugar, delicious. I stared at the coin,
unable to credit my luck. I had enough for at least five *pepitos,* if
I didn't buy the medium size.

"This bit of paper I'm going to give you, look after it carefully." He came close to me and said in a low voice in my ear,
"When you plan on leaving those two witches, call this number, Delmira. We'll get you out of Agustini. We'll put plenty of
distance between them and you. On the other side of the sea,
where they can't bug you."

I took the paper in a hand sweaty with nervousness and started to run. I crossed the whole market without stopping once. I didn't even stop to buy a *pepito*. I shot into the house, straight to my balcony and the plant pot with pieces of broken mirror set in its sides, in which grew huge blossoms, obscenely red, whose name I can't now recall. In the soil of the pot I kept the key to the little chest that belonged at the bottom of my wardrobe. I scratched at the soil urgently and pulled out the key. Just as urgently I grabbed the little chest and deposited in it what remained of my money, plus the coin and piece of paper I'd just gotten from the vendor, without reading it or even unfolding it. Then I locked the box and put it back in its hiding place, where nobody could find it. I raked the black soil of the plant pot with my nails so that there remained no trace of my activity, except for my blackened nails. All the time I hadn't let go, even for an instant, of the head scarf, squeezing it tightly under my arm against my chest. The pole I'd left lying on the floor of my bedroom. I came out, carrying both presents, eager to find Mama quickly, as if somebody might take them off me before I found her. I thought she'd be on the veranda overlooking the garden or by the riverbank, but I couldn't find her in either place. As I came back across the garden, I felt curious about my purchase and I unwrapped the package. I wanted to find out if I could make the head scarf fly, so I opened it up, spread it out, and shook it vigorously, watching it fill with air. Then I let it go, but it fell gracelessly to the ground. I dusted it clean as best I could and wrapped it up again. I retraced my steps and kept on searching for Mama. When I saw her, she'd just come out of her room and was about to sit in the rocking chair, as languid as usual.

"Here!" I said to her.

She made no answer.

Before accepting what I had to offer, she opened her fan and fanned herself, at the same time rocking the chair. She took the fruit-pole and checked it carefully.

"Leave it in my room. See if it fits in. It's really long."

My choice didn't seem to go down too well with her. I ran to do as I'd been told and came back. I stood beside her. Without opening her eyes, she said, "What do you want?"

"I brought you a couple of things, Mama. I want to give you another present."

"Present? The pole was what you owed me, don't you think?" she replied, still without opening her eyes.

I gave her the package and she opened it at once. I noticed a shock of surprise when she saw the contents.

"Where did you get this?"

"I went to the market with Dulce. Then she got lost and I went looking for a present for you. I got the pole first in the hardware place and then I saw the stall with the shawls. I bought it for you with the money Uncle Gus gives me when he comes on visits. I've saved it all. Don't you like it? If you don't like it, there's no problem! I'll go change it."

My explanation calmed her and the scarf couldn't fail to please her, it was so lovely. She ran her hand over my hand in a careless imitation of a caress.

"It's very pretty."

Old Skin-and-Bones, as the vendor had called her, came dashing over to us, carrying a broom in her right hand, with her arm extended, as if the broom were a weapon.

"And what's that?" she asked, halting abruptly on seeing the scarf in Mama's arms.

"Isn't it pretty?" said Mama, smiling.

"Pretty, for sure. Where did it come from?"

She listened only to the first part of the story and then carried on with her business, not staying to hear Mama's version to the end, a version much more elaborate and far less true than my own. She went off, broom at the ready, hurried and stiff-backed, en route to some arduous battle.

I'd have liked to interrupt her. I'd like to have flourished my long fruit-pole and challenged her to a duel. Her bit of a stick against my fruit-picker, her false antiquity against my overlooked infancy, her military mind against my sense of joy. It really had brought me joy, my trip through the tent of scarves, wraps, and shawls that the vendor had built for me, even if only for a few minutes. O how happy I felt!

But my desire to challenge her and the explosion of joy that threatened to burst my lungs came collapsing back down to earth, like the scarf in the garden, when, seconds later, Dulce burst in, all upset, her face tense, like a raging meteorite aimed directly at me. She scolded me for getting lost in the market, as if it had been my fault, and after her came Grandma to scold her for having left me alone, and after her came Mama, saying that it didn't really matter, going on and on, pulling at Grandma's sleeve, getting into a snit because she was paying too much attention to me and Dulce, and Grandma turning on Mama, saying that the Gypsies or the Chinese could have easily stolen me away, and Dulce still attacking me tooth and nail, and then Grandma giving it to Dulce, because, in addition to not having taken proper care of me and exposing me to a thousand imaginary perils, she had forgotten the last of the three errands, had bought the wrong thing on the second, and had let herself be charged double the actual price on the first.

4

My Pain, Their Hammock

The next day was Sunday and the household followed its regular routine for the day. On the seventh day we dolled ourselves up in our finery and went to the nine o'clock Mass, the last one of the morning, where we mingled with the better sort of people. After mass we ate breakfast at the house of the parish priest, on a lovely, cool terrace, surrounded by plants. From the roof of beams and tiles hung birdcages and hanging baskets always filled with flowers and buds on the point of opening into more flowers. The floor was mosaic, the chairs were of wood. On the long table was spread a white tablecloth embroidered in bright colors by the tireless nuns. They also were responsible for the exquisite Sunday breakfast: tamales, *atole,* enchiladas, meat pies, sweet pastry, and bread rolls, all baked in the convent kitchen. Three of the nuns breakfasted with us, the ones charged with looking after the priest. They dressed in light gray, with a starched white veil on their heads, as stiff as a cap. The priest himself, a tall, dark, handsome man of strapping build, who wore delicately framed spectacles which lent him an inexplicable air of sympathy, was the idol of the nuns, the object of their profane devotion, their private god. They were also fond of us, and on Sundays we formed part of their happy family. They trotted here and there, attending to everybody, and when they sat down they felt responsible for keeping the conversation lively. They never stopped talking, telling us stories, gossip, legends, and scandalous rumors, until it was time for them to argue over the embroidery of the tablecloth. That moment always came. Then they forgot about us completely and pushed plates, cups, mugs, bowls, napkins, and cutlery to the other side of the table, prattling on about where another flower was needed, more branches, another bunch of grapes, or what petal should go on what stem, what leaf on what branch, disagreeing among themselves, each defending her own opinion against the others with a glib tongue and even using a fingernail on the tablecloth to demonstrate what shape a leaf ought to take or where a petal was missing, and then proceeding to smooth out the scratched cloth with the edge of a spoon to prove that this new addition had destroyed the harmony of the whole composition, and on and on.

The rest of us got up from the table, but they remained, arguing their points, getting more heated every minute, until they literally climbed onto the table, all dignity gone, crawling around, disputing one detail after another of the cloth, somehow managing not to soil their stiff veils with sauces and coffee dregs. Then the priest marched off with Mama and me to his jeep, Grandma disappeared, and we drove out of town to one of the nearby ranches, to participate in the mass. Both of us acted as his assistants. During the mass itself, I passed around the collection plate and Mama cleaned up the sacristy. Before and after the service, she helped the priest with his robes and packed them carefully in the priest's small suitcase before we filed off to our next destination, which might or might not have a church or a chapel. The priest was so eager to say Mass that he would have done it in the middle of a swamp or in the burning sun or the pouring rain.

When it came to preaching at Mass, the priest had no equal, but en route it was Mama who wouldn't let him get a word in

edgewise. I don't know what she said to him. The dusty roads
were in appalling condition, the jeep bounced around endlessly,
squeaking and squealing, and as they had sat me in the back I
couldn't hear a word. But it gave me a good feeling to see her so
animated, unlike the rest of the week. She had awoken from her
lethargy. She had flowered. She was gesticulating, moving her
hands, her whole body, with grace and assurance. He'd turn to
look at her and nod his head in agreement or shake it in disagree-
ment, and then immediately return his attention to the winding
road, with its potholes, ridges, and dangerous rocks that could
have holed the gas tank, which in fact they had done on one
occasion. That time we were stuck without gas, because it had
all poured out of the damaged tank, but we were lucky because
on that little-traveled road we came across another vehicle, a
wagon loaded with sugarcane—like ours, it was good for little
else than filling the jungle with its roaring and bucking—but at
least it rescued us. Mama and the priest sat behind, climbing up
on top of the load, and they put me inside with the driver. I could
never forget that trip, even though I slept all the way home,
because Mama arrived home covered in scratches from the cane
and it was a week before she quit complaining of her numerous
pains. Every time she let out a whine, Grandma would turn on
her with "But why didn't you put the kid up top? Nothing would
have happened to her. Kids are made of rubber." And every time
she said it, I'd be overcome with shame for my thoughtlessness
and for having hurt Mama in such an ugly way.

After the third Mass, I invariably fell fast asleep as we drove
home, rocked by so much bumping and tired out by so much
sun and dust and, if it was the rainy season, by the endless slith-
ering in the mud. My nap coincided with the rest period of the
adults. Half asleep, I would realize the car had stopped. I'd hear
them get out. Then I'd snuggle up to get more comfortable in
the backseat which I shared with the priest's suitcase, and get on

with my long, worry-free nap. But on the Sunday I'm talking about, the underside of the jeep hit something, as it emerged into a clearing, and I got a nasty knock on the head and woke up completely. I opened my eyes and saw them getting out, Father Lima first. With a courtesy I hadn't seen in him before, he came around to open Mama's door, took her by the hand, and without his letting go of it the pair of them set off toward the river. Instead of nestling back down again, I craned forward as far as I could to see what happened next, where they were going off to. On the dashboard of the jeep lay the priest's spectacles. His face looked naked as he laughed loudly for some unknown reason. He led Mama by the hand to the trunk of the next tree, rolled up his soutane, and climbed up into the branches as fast as a cat. From up there he threw something down to Mama and came down as agilely as he'd gone up. Then he took off his black soutane, revealing his naked chest and black tailored pants, which I'd never imagined as being under the battered soutane he wore in all weathers, even the most intense heat. With his dreary robe gone, without spectacles and shirt, this tropical James Dean gave pursuit to Mama, dressed in her white skirt of light, airy cotton. He tried to snatch away from her the bulky object he'd thrown down from the tree, but she wouldn't let him have it and, laughing, struggled to escape. They were playing like two children until he won, getting the object away from her, and then she chased him, trying to get it back. She grabbed him by the waist, then he held her with one of his arms and put one end of the object they were playing with into her hand. It was a woven hammock. They moved apart, stretching it out. He tied his end to the branch he'd just climbed and then came over to Mama to help her tie her end to a nearby tree, a handsome laurel whose roots were fed by the powerful river.

There he sat down on a fallen log, undid his shoelaces, took off his socks and pants, and passed them to Mama. He wasn't wearing underpants, which astonished me. Mama took off her dress and settled it with his clothes in the crook of a branch in the first tree. She wasn't wearing panties, either. She removed her bra, gave a little scream, and in her bare feet joined him in the hammock. Together now and naked, they began to kiss and caress each other. I huddled down in my seat. I'd seen all I wanted to see. What were the pair of them doing without their clothes on? What did they think they were up to? It had to be a sin, what they were doing. I could hear them as if they were talking right into my ear. The heavy breathing, the exclamations, the groans, Mama saying "Now" and "Don't be stingy, give it to me" and then "More, more, give me more" and the priest "Here it is then," for hours or what seemed like hours. I felt desperate. What they were doing was shattering something inside me, ripping me apart, plundering me. Maybe it wasn't a sin, but for me it was evil, the ultimate evil, the very incarnation of evil. I detested them.

Suddenly I got an inspiration: it would be less painful if I could see them, instead of just listening to their insufferable moaning. I straightened up in the seat. It was true; their groans sounded less loud now that I could see them, but the horrid truth was that what I saw left me totally deaf. There was an intense buzzing in my ears, as if my head was going to explode. Mama was facedown, hanging from the hammock, which instead of being extended in leisurely fashion between two points, as before, now had both ends with her upper body draped over the top of the hammock, which, instead of being stretched comfortably wide, was now wrapped tight as a rope to support her bending frame, as she stood on the ground and braced herself. He was behind her, clutching at her bum, battering his body against hers, with an expression of pain on his face as he turned it toward me, his eyes shut, his mouth open, totally wrapped up in himself. The rest of their bodies presented themselves to me in profile. She turned her face toward him, making her posture even more grotesque, in a gesture of pain that hurt me in my own stomach. She opened her mouth and then he spit on her, leaving on her a considerable amount of saliva. What were they doing? Once again I sank back into the car seat. I thought about getting out and starting to run, but I was paralyzed by horror, horror at the whole thing. I imagined myself getting out of the car. Getting out through the jeep's window so as not to disturb them by banging the door. I'd walk toward the river, my two feet in mud, more mud at every step, and I'd sink into it till I couldn't take another step forward because I couldn't pull my feet out of the mud. At every moment I was sinking deeper, quickly. I could hear them again.

"No, no, not that way."

"Here it is, take it, you like it."

"No, no."

"Either that way or nothing at all."

"Don't be like that. Give it to me. More."

"Here it is then."

And I didn't dare call out, "Save me! Help me! The swamp is swallowing me!" Then the mud covered my mouth, first my mouth, then my nose, filling them with its filth. Then my eyes. All of me. The swamp was swallowing me at the same time as sleep was overcoming me.

They woke me up when we arrived at the next place for Mass. I thought I must have dreamt the whole thing, when I saw him so smiling and cordial, so orderly and handsome; and her, so much in control of herself, so correct and so full of self-assurance. So many "take its" and "mores" couldn't have come out of their two mouths. In a few minutes I'd persuaded myself that I'd imagined it all, and I was thoroughly ashamed of myself.

At this ranch there was a slight contretemps. Somebody had stolen the hosts and the consecration wine. The priest said it was no big deal, none of it had been blessed, nobody would suffer under a curse, they shouldn't worry about it, in itself the theft didn't amount to much, but, hopefully, the culprit enjoyed the taste of the hosts and didn't get a nasty headache from the consecration wine. But he couldn't say Mass because they hadn't brought another batch of hosts or any wine in the suitcase. He heard some confessions, visited a little old lady, they gave us each a delicious fried patty of lizard meat, and we turned back home, worn out, the same as every Sunday, unspeaking and dying of hunger, because the patty had only sharpened our appetites.

The priest dropped us off at home and went his way. Mama and I had a meal in our usual silence, while Grandma complained about how late it was. "How come you guys get back so late? You're going to do yourselves an injury! Of course, I've nothing against you helping the priest, but think about the kid. It's almost suppertime and you're just having lunch!" Then she complained about her feet. About whatever.

Once we'd eaten, we dressed ourselves up and took a stroll to the Alameda. Around the central bandstand, the men were walking in one direction, the women in another. The town band played the same numbers as always, once again off-key as we'd come to expect. My nanny, Dulce, and I did a couple of turns around the bandstand with Mama and then came home, as it was my bedtime. As soon as we got back, Grandma let down her hair, Dulce started to comb it, and I lay down in my hammock. Not even for an instant did I think about the trick my imagination had apparently played on me that afternoon, nor did I pay any attention to Grandma's story. Instead, I recalled the piece of paper that the vendor of shawls, scarves, and rebozos had given me. I was burning to read it. What was in it? I pushed aside what my imagination had seen the priest and Mama do, because I couldn't bear to think of it. But I had to fight it off hard so that it wouldn't get me in its ferocious hold. It was intolerable.

Today is the first time that I have recalled these details. I accept now that I didn't dream it, that I wasn't guilty of having produced it. It was those two who produced it, and I witnessed it by mistake. Certainly it wasn't my imagination that hung them so grotesquely in the hammock or drove the weight of the man against the naked buttocks of the woman, or made them groan so desperately. They had repeated that scene many a Sunday. Maybe, trusting to my habit of sleeping deeply, they took me along in the car so that nobody, neither Grandma nor the other parishioners, would suspect. I no longer blame myself for it, nor do I blame them. I too would have loved the priest, and if I'd been him I wouldn't have resisted the charms of my mother.

Finally, today, I can take a deep breath. I'm not the monster who dreamed up an abominable scene to wound the heart and body of a little girl. Delmira, it wasn't you. Take it easy, Delmira, take it easy.

5

The Ladies Fight

On Monday, after I'd gotten back from school and eaten supper, I took advantage of Dulce's inattention to scurry off to my wardrobe. I quickly opened my little chest, eager to read the piece of paper it contained. I took it out, but it was hardly in my hands when I heard them all coming toward my room, arguing among themselves. So I hastily locked the chest and hid the paper in the palm of my hand. They came in like a whirlwind, Dulce, my mother, my grandmother, Ofelia, who came to do the cleaning, and Petra, who came to do the washing and ironing. Instead of folding up the paper to stop them seeing it, I started to roll it up. Nobody turned to notice me, but I felt that at any moment any one of them might cast an acid, burning glance at what I was doing. So I rolled it up as fast as I could, as tight as I could make it, while they went on arguing loudly about my crinoline skirt. Dulce was saying that it was badly washed, that it had a stain. Petra was saying that she'd left it spotless, and that if it had a stain, it was Ofelia's fault, because she was the one who'd hung it in my wardrobe. Then, without pausing in their avowals that yes, it was dirty and that no, it wasn't dirty, they pulled the skirt out of the wardrobe to examine it, opening up the balcony windows a little to cast some light on the matter. I kept working on my roll, which I now had the impression was enormous because I couldn't manage to complete the job.

There certainly was a stain on the crinoline. It looked like a dirty fingermark, or an earth stain. "Poor Ofelia," I thought when I saw it, "now they've really started something." Petra announced that she wasn't going to wash it again, not for anything, that she wasn't going to all the trouble of starching and ironing it all over again, because it was Ofelia's fault. Then poor Ofelia, with her voice trembling, said, "It doesn't matter, madam. I didn't dirty it but I'll wash it." This infuriated Petra. "So, why don't you admit it then? Tell the truth. You had it in your filthy paws after you'd been picking your nose." Then Dulce waded in, saying that an idiot like Ofelia would be bound to burn it with the iron and that Petra had better do it. The argument was getting heated. Dulce, whose complexion was yellow (her face, typical of the Otomi tribe, had an oriental cast to it), had by now turned red and was totally blowing her lid. Nobody was showing any self-control.

"In my opinion, there's no need to make such a fuss over a little matter," I heard myself saying, with a new confidence now that my paper was totally rolled up, hidden like a tube between my fingers. "I know what we should do. After all, nobody's going to see the stain. The crinoline goes under my dress. Once I put my dress on, who'll know the difference?"

"In this house nobody goes dirty," brayed Grandma. "If you want to go dirty, you'd better do it somewhere else. You are the limit!"

"It's your fault, Dulce," my mother accused her. "The kid is half wild because you let her get away with—"

I saw that the storm was about to burst, and since nobody was paying me any attention I slipped away toward the garden without uttering a peep, to see what the seller of shawls, veils, scarves, and rebozos had written down for me. But I'd barely

gotten my two feet outside the door when the storm broke over
me again.

"It's all your fault, and you don't care! You're heartless!"
my mother was yelling.

"I'm talking to you, and you go turn your back on me,"
added my grandmother.

"Shitty kid, they're going to blame me now all because of
you," howled Dulce. "Where you going?"

"I bet it was her," accused Petra. "She was the one who
dirtied it with her own filthy hands."

Ofelia was also glaring at me with rage, as if I was the one
responsible for everything that had gone wrong in her life.

At first I wasn't even going to say "I've a right to speak,"
because I was used to these irrational outbursts of foul temper
and I knew they never took me into account, anyway. But now
they were all staring at me in silence and I felt obliged to mutter
some explanation.

"But nobody was talking to me . . . It's got nothing to do
with me . . . I'm sorry, Grandma, I didn't realize you wanted to
say something to me . . . I was just going out to get some fresh
air, because it was starting to get hot in the room."

"Get hot! . . . nothing gets you hot, you cold-blooded
snake," said Grandma. "Nothing ever matters to you. If it was
up to you, you'd go around dressed like one of those Indians at
the market."

Years later I would confirm the truth of her words, but at
that moment I gave absolute proof to her allegation of my cold-
bloodedness. In front of their infuriated eyes, I opened up my
divine roll of paper and read it. All it had on it was a telephone
number, which I memorized. I rolled it up again between finger
and thumb, and went through the motions of raising it calmly to
my lips like a cigarette.

My grandmother shrugged her shoulders, as if I was a lost cause, and turned her back on me. Then she resumed her discussion of the unfortunate crinoline and kept it up till darkness fell and it was time for her to bar the door, get out the combs, and start telling her tales.

6

Grandmother's Story

"Well, you see," began Grandma, "after the rebels came to the farm for the third time and cleared out all our provisions, and raped the women servants, and killed one or two of the men servants, though none of them had put up any resistance—not showing resistance was part of the deal we'd struck with the rebels, so they'd leave us in peace, me, my mother, and my three sisters, that is—Grandfather decided that he'd seen enough of their shenanigans, and that we'd better move out and go live in our house in town. That's how we came to be where we are today, even though it's not a patch on the house at the farm. Our kitchen here can't compare with the one we had out there, either; it had a brick oven for bread and twelve burners heated by coal. The living room here is piddling compared to the farm's, with its dance floor. And these bedrooms are poky beside those at the farm, where each of us had a dressing room to ourselves almost the size of Delmira's room. In fact, her room used to be a dressing room when we first moved here and we four sisters shared it, fighting over every inch, fitting in our collars and ribbons and other bits and pieces, which I'm not going to mention now, for making our dresses, because back then things weren't like they are nowadays, when girls wrap themselves in a bit of cloth and

call it a proper dress. The kitchen was different too, and the
bedrooms, not to mention the gardens and the patios, and the
fountains my father had had built. He'd brought over some tall
black workers to haul in special stone from unheard-of places with
unpronounceable names and he had it polished till it shone like
mirrors. There were orchards as well and an avenue, and a prom-
enade we'd had built through the cocoa plantation, and grassy
paths bordered with exotic flowers . . .

"Around our way there were hardly any federal forces. There
had been outbreaks of insurrection here and there, among people
with nothing better to do than act the bully and go looting this
and that. At the time of the Revolution that's all the rebels were
around here—bullies, and troublemakers, and good-for-nothings.
They'd heard there was a revolution in progress, so they all
jumped on the bandwagon and went crazy, without any idea of
duty or fear or knowledge of how to organize, unlike the real
revolutionaries who were jumping on and off trains, busily or-
chestrating an attack or the capture of a town or a victory, under
leaders with grand ambitions and the great courage needed to
achieve them. The rebels here went around killing one another.
They didn't need the federal forces to have enemies. They had
plenty among themselves.

"One time when they came to the farm, their chief—
though he didn't look like much of a leader, a tall, redheaded,
bony fellow, with a very pale complexion and a roguish look
constantly on his face, as if he was laughing up his sleeve at the
whole thing, and dressed in a style that boggles the imagination—
that day he was wearing a nightdress with lace trimmings and
hand-embroidered ribbons that I'd once seen an aunt of mine
wearing—I don't know whether she was from my father's side
or my mother's—a sick woman, never well for two minutes
together, but anyway, there he was in her nightie that he'd half
torn to shreds, though he'd patched it here and there with the

colored ribbons, and over the top of it he'd put the stole of some
bishop, using the fringed ends to make phony epaulettes—well,
this chief, as I was saying, was standing at the top of the steps, in
front of the main door of the house, negotiating with my father
for the price of our safety. We'd already agreed to certain things
so that they wouldn't touch us: first, not to fight them; second,
to pay a ransom which kept getting bigger and bigger. They were
throwing figures back and forth, along with banknotes and hard
looks, and while this leader, as I was saying, was doing his negotiating, one of his mob laid hands on my sister Florinda. Mama
let out a scream and Papa was informed immediately. So he took
one of the bundles of banknotes in his hand, waved it in the face
of the redheaded leader, and, with one of the matches he always
carried in his pocket, set fire to it.

"'I'd sooner burn my money,' he said furiously, 'before I'd
give it to a man who breaks his word.'

"The redheaded chief answered with a disturbing laugh. He
found everything funny.

"'And who told you I don't keep my word?' he replied.
'I'm so much bound by my word that I'll keep it with regard to
your women, even though you've broken yours.'

"'Who told me!?' glowered Papa, unable to see he was
putting us all in danger. 'Who told me! You, sir, have just heard
that one of your men has had the temerity to lay a disrespectful
hand on my daughters, and you can ask me that!'

"'Don't jump to conclusions,' answered the chief, still grinning. 'Hey, bring that stupid girl-molester over here.'

"Immediately they brought over a dark-complexioned,
filthy-looking ruffian who hadn't combed his hair in decades.

"'So it was you, our famous Refugio,' said the chief. 'What
got into you, man? Hadn't we agreed that we weren't going to
lay a finger on these nice young ladies and their mother?' The
ruffian nodded his head, almost without understanding a thing,

a complete brute of a man, unable to figure out that two and two make more than three. 'I want you to apologize to this gentleman, and tell him that if you did brush against his daughter, it was to get rid of a nasty spider that was crawling on her hair. Or where was it exactly that you touched her, eh?'

"The brute, who really didn't look as if he could speak, pointed to his own buttocks.

"'Oh, there! How horrible, to have an insect crawling there! Well, sir, this other insect will receive twelve lashes right now across his bare back, even though he was only removing a bug from your daughter's person. That's what he was doing. That's why he dared to brush against the girl, not out of a lack of respect, but almost from an excess of courtesy. The lash! Bring me the lash! Off with your shirt, man!'

"The brute took off his shirt with a docility that was positively animal. Another of the men brought an enormous lash tricked out with sharp bits of metal that they'd found at God knows whose ranch. On our farm we didn't beat our Indians with things like that. They tied him to the trunk of a kapok tree that grew by the main door of the house, to one side of the central stairway, with his arms over his head, and right there in front us the chief lashed him, not twelve but at least thirty times.

"Then he let the lash drop, went up the stairway, with his nightie even more tattered than before, one shoulder half out of it, and his curly hair all tousled and his face on fire with his efforts, and addressed Papa with a relaxed smile.

"'There! I think that'll do. I believe you've seen I'm a man of my word. And as I think you are as well, I'm going to make our deal a reality. Come here, young lady!' he said to my sister Florinda. 'Please stand on this stone.'

"On both sides of the stairway there were banisters of quarried stone which ended in a veranda with a pair of low stone columns. It was on one of these that he asked Florinda to stand.

"'Now, you sir,' he said to Papa, 'are going to give no orders to your men. I swear to you that I'm going to show no disrespect to your daughter or do her any harm. I'm only going to give you a chance to recover your honor as a gentleman. Will you pass me one of your matches?'

"Papa passed him a match, and the box to light it, signaling to Florinda to do as the man said. She was dressed in a lovely white dress with a sort of apron of tulle in front. The guy took hold of the edge of the apron and set fire to it and let it fall against the dress. Immediately the dress caught fire from contact with the flames. Mama screamed. My grandmother, María del Mar, screamed even louder. My other sisters squealed like animals in pain. But I did something quite embarrassing: I started to laugh. The redheaded chief and I couldn't contain our guffaws. Then he took the bishop's stole from his chest and put out the flames on the dress with it, stifling them with the gilded embroidery.

"'I'm afraid, dear sir, that I've had to take from your daughter what you sent up in flames. If I'm not mistaken, you burnt a quarter of the ransom you were offering. By your reckoning, that was the price of this girl's safety, because right from the start you said you were paying me just for your daughters. Respect for the mother and the grandmother was a generous bonus my men and I were throwing in free.' My father was deathly pale, scared out of his wits. 'Forgive me if I contradict you, but I suspect that your lovely Florinda is worth a lot more than you were offering for her. By my reckoning what you were giving only covered a corner of her dress. And that's what I burnt. Not one piece more. Do you agree with my calculations?' Papa nodded his head. 'So the next time I come through here, you'd better pay me the full price, because if you don't I'll only respect what you're paying for. Let that be our gentlemen's agreement, eh? Okay?'

"The mob had watched the burning of Florinda's dress without uttering a sound. But the minute their chief stopped speaking, they started to shout, bellowing at the top of their lungs, and dashed into the house, while their musicians played drums and guitars as loud as they could from the garden. We remained on the terrace. Inside the house, a wild party was soon in progress. Night fell and they were still inside. Finally they came stumbling out, lighting their way with candles.

"'You're not going to stay and sleep here?' asked my idiot of a grandmother.

"'We wouldn't sleep in this pigsty, madam, thanks very much all the same,' said the chief sarcastically, now wearing bits and pieces of my mother's and grandmother's clothes over my father's best pair of trousers. Then he climbed on his horse and disappeared, followed by his drunken gang.

"The next day we moved here. We never went back to the farm, because Mama got sick again and died a short while after. Died just as she'd lived, without ever cutting her hair even once. When she let it down, it reached to her ankles, you know. Papa followed her to the grave in next to no time, and Grandma María del Mar did the same a few weeks later. So the four of us were left to fend for ourselves, though we did have the help of Papa's brother, who managed our inheritance with absolute honesty. Though only because we didn't give him time to steal it from us. Then, as fast as we could, each of us found a husband. My three sisters had first-rate luck, because, I suppose, they were the only ones from the upper classes still around here at that time. Three good husbands they picked out for themselves. And me? Well, I got what I got, a complete good-for-nothing. The only memorable thing he ever did was die early. That's what happens when you're the last one. You get the leftovers."

7

The Birds

The following Sunday we didn't join the priest on his rural jaunt, because that morning, around eight o'clock, all the birds, regardless of their mode of flight, whether they moved in wide circles or just enormous curves before gliding slowly onward, or rocked to and fro and leaned to one side in mid-flight, or floated low over field and swamp, their wings slightly above the horizontal plane, or executed a variety of short, rapid flutterings or flew by alternating fluttering with gliding or made a habit of hanging suspended in the air, beating their wings and coming down feet-first to fish, or soared upward in great circles—one and all came tumbling beakfirst to the ground, unable to get airborne again. One after another, they opened their wings to fly but all came back down to earth, walking on their feet like defenseless creatures in need of shoes. The roadrunners didn't notice the change, nor did the ducks which lived hidden among the rushes of the swamp, stuck in the mud, scratching the backs of the fishes. But tick-eaters couldn't get off the ground and back onto the necks of the cows, and the American tree-climber, which winds its way up the trunks of trees and then drops to the base of the next tree, couldn't even flutter a short distance to help itself climb to safety. All around, the birds made efforts to take off, but they ended up falling back to earth, sometimes beating their wings but not always, as if some heavy air were suddenly circulating through their bones, an air laden with water or weighted with earth, almost sandy.

Before our eyes, the cats and dogs launched into a gory butchery, glutting themselves on this luxurious banquet, till they were sated and smeared with the blood of the birds. Before long we saw even eagles harassed by quadrupeds. Hummingbirds, beating their wings a thousand times a minute, couldn't get off the ground, buffeting their attackers with their wings before dying in a mixture of saliva and blood. We dashed to defend the birds, while others stashed the rarer specimens in cages or what they could improvise as cages, bundling in this repugnant treasure before my eyes.

The hourly bus had not yet come into town, but when it did, sounding the horn to get the birds to move aside and give it some space, its luggage rack was packed with a multitude of exotic birds I'd never seen before. The highways were infested with creatures that should have been flying. It was one thing to crush common zanates and guitos under your wheels but a far different thing to run down a green-billed toucan or a white-horned owl or an immense scarlet guayacama, a parrot, a scissor-bird, a lily-galloper, an owl from the bell tower with its white, heart-shaped face, a handsome quetzal with its long tail, an eagle or a kingfisher. The passengers unloaded their luggage from the bus, but it wasn't easy to find a place to put it, for the birds on the roof joined the already thronged sidewalk, cluttered with love-birds and pigeons, trogons and cuclillos, cezontles and tanagers and red cardinals. The patios of houses were also thronged with various birds, terraces and rooftops likewise, and if the tiles were sloping, the birds eventually fell off them down onto the ground with a distressing gracelessness, for by now they had lost even the capacity to flutter. They were walking along the sidewalks and the paths of the park in a stately fashion, and just as they had previously formed flocks in the sky, so now they formed them down on the earth, strutting around in serried ranks of feathers, which made it awkward for people to get around the town, as the birds closed ranks impenetrably, and the people had to take other routes where other birds, less given to parading about, left spaces on the ground.

We chained up the dogs, we shut the cats in the house as best we could. Mothers spanked some children for tormenting the defenseless birds and shooed away the more aggressive birds from other, more peace-loving children. Traffic was brought to a standstill, whether motor-driven or horse-drawn. We tried not to worry about what had happened, as if it were quite normal to live in a town where there were more feathers than dust and mud. The teacher from the secondary school borrowed nets from the fishermen and organized his students to rescue the birds that were drowning after falling into the river.

Mass was interrupted by the calls of birds that filled the atrium and the floor of the church, some calls resembling those of frogs, others harsh and heartbreaking, repeated *cla-acks,* or nonstop cacklings or a chatter of castanets that froze your soul. Or *flick-a, flick-a,* or *wick-wick,* or a deep *uchrrrrr* followed by a sharp *pi,* or a gruff *chifti-chifti,* or sometimes a slow, piglike grunting, an oink, or two or three sadder, more desolate sighings that died away gradually in intensity and rhythm. Or a *switsit* or was it a *psiit* or a *siist* with a rising inflection? Then a *hooy-see,* a *peet-see-oh,* sharp and explosive, a *tee-dee-day,* a *chur-wee,* a musical *troo-lee,* but since there wasn't a single specimen of the gray musketeer whose song resembles the priest's "Joseph'n Mary, Joseph'n Mary" around to help him, he couldn't concentrate on the ceremony.

The breakfast likewise was disrupted by the same hullaba-loo. Wordlessly the sisters gazed at their caged birds, till one of

them said, "Well, if it's up to me, they can fly away." Another
then opened the cages, but only one sparrow tried to escape and
it crashed down onto the floor of the terrace, like a small bag of
dried corn, and severely injured its beak. From the priest's garden a rare black and white owl stared at us with its enormous
eyes. Its back and face were black and it never once took its eyes
off us, continually going *hooey-oo-oo,* a dolorous song that hardly
went well with the morning light. Now and then our talk was
interrupted by a monotonous, grating *k-rrrk* or *g-rrrk,* like a giant
grasshopper's, but actually coming from a toucan. That morning there was no chatter about the state of the tablecloth; the
vegetation embroidered on it was allowed to remain undisturbed.
The nuns quickly cleared the table, and the priest, visibly shaken,
mounted his horse and trotted off as fast as he could, picking his
way through feathery obstacles, and we didn't see him again for
the next three days.

The picoleznas that often hang head-down from branches
were shattered unmercifully on the ground because they had
landed on their unprotected, soft heads as they tried to change
position. The odd zacua or tanager had avoided destruction,
because they shared the huge, socklike nests hanging from the
kapok trees. But as evening came on, we heard them fighting
among themselves with such violence that when children put
their hands in the nest to rescue them, they pulled out birds
without eyes, savagely pecked, already dead. They had fought
to the death over these tiny areas of safety.

For many children these were glory days. They made more
noise than the birds, jumping and scurrying up and down the
town, as if the falling of the birds were some kind of fun party, a
holiday of beaks and blood that excited them beyond the limits
of self-control. Youngsters, even the young teacher at the secondary school, strutted around the streets with the air of heroes,

displaying their most recent rescues from the rivers and giving first aid to the wounded birds on the town streets.

The next morning, as simply as they had fallen to earth, the birds soared upward again, as if nothing had happened, as if they knew nothing of the thousands of corpses littering the streets and highways. We were obliged to give the town a thorough cleanup, before it started to stink. Grandma suggested we stew some of the birds that were still lukewarm. She proposed we all make a *mole* sauce to get rid of the bad taste that Sunday had left in our mouths, claiming that it was an outrageous waste to throw the birds away, that it was really a sin to be so unthrifty, because among the corpses there were dozens of blue-footed ducks, whose flesh tasted even better than a turtle's. The priest wasn't around to say either way, lost on God knows what road. But the doctor said that the behavior of the birds might be indicative of some sickness that could be passed on to humans, and that the best thing was to get rid of the corpses as hygienically as possible, by cremating them in a huge bonfire on the outskirts of town. So those who had earlier been the saviors of the birds were transformed by this medical edict into inquisitorial lowlifes, burning the victims they had once hoped to save. All we kids attended the bonfire, from start to finish, even though the stink was disgusting. When the fire was extinguished, we were left without a single lovely, showy feather; only the longer sorts of beaks and bones remained. The sole trace of that vanished beauty was a pile of dark ashes.

Throughout the week, the town heard a mild rumor, gossip that the jungle was being cleared on a ranch recently purchased by the governor. They were ripping out trees with cranes and excavators to clear a space for pastureland. They said the roads were jammed with trucks loaded with timber and that the area had been stripped bare, as if a single tree had never grown there. "That's why the birds fell to the ground" was the whisper.

On Saturday, at the market, there appeared stalls with feathers for sale and large plates of clay and plaster trimmed with feathers. Instead of using paints, the Indians had decided to color them with feathers, somehow sticking them onto the plates. I wanted to buy some reddish ones and some with almost metallic colors, but Grandma scolded me. "Didn't you hear what the doctor said? Are you really in a rush to die? You're a dimwit, you know that?"

8

The Volcano

The following Sunday the volcano that had been dormant for centuries sent out prolonged, dense columns of smoke. It was impossible to leave home because the air was thick with corrosive material that hurt our eyes and throats. If people were obliged to leave the house, they had to cover their mouths with a handkerchief, which was soon darkened with soot, as if they'd put it near smoke escaping from an oil fire.

We all stayed steadfastly indoors, with the balconies and doors tight shut, suffocating in the heat, with the ceiling fans whirring, because nobody could stand the burning air outside. Mass was canceled, said the rumor going from house to house. The Indians didn't come down from the hills to attend it. The market was dead, the streets fit only for ghosts. Agustini had lost its identity, had turned into a vacuum.

We did not go to the priest's breakfast. No doubt the nuns stuffed their bellies all day long with tamales, while I, stretched in my hammock, indifferent to the town's boredom, was devouring *Robin Hood*. I finished the book in a single day.

But for everybody else the day meant only discomfort and suffocation. Our houses were designed to be left open. The rooms were built individually, giving onto open-air patios and passageways, so some families spent the whole day in the kitchen, to avoid movement, while others darted from one room to another, with blackened handkerchiefs over their noses. The teacher at the secondary school printed out on the school's stencil machine a series of instructions to be followed in case the activity of the volcano increased. He advised us to leave Agustini at the first sounding of the alarm; the church bells would ring out three-two, three-two fives times over, and he explained how to sew face masks which would allow us to leave home, if it came to that, and listed the things we should take with us: containers of water, packets of crackers, flashlights, candles, and, if possible, a radio, with batteries included.

His instructions filled three typed pages and included two illustrations: a sketch of the homemade face mask and another of the evacuation routes. He gave a supplementary list of things to carry if we had to abandon the town, for example, blankets and hammocks for sleeping, and urged us to load as few goods as possible into our cars in order to leave room for as many people as possible, regardless (underlined) of their race, age, or sex.

My grandmother said these instructions were pure nonsense, my mother said she couldn't be bothered with them, but Dulce did show some real interest, so I read them out loud to her. We were the only two in the house who knew what the teacher had recommended, and we both decided simultaneously that if the volcano was determined to swamp us in lava or bury us in ashes, the only recourse was to remove ourselves at the first opportunity to another town, as every other measure seemed pointless.

In the afternoon a wind began to blow and I think it scared us all. Branches came crashing down from trees. The highway was blocked by two uprooted trees. But the smoke from the volcano was dispersed, disappearing as unexpectedly as it had appeared.

9

The Coffee

The following Sunday the coffee beans and the cacao pods which had recently sprouted fell off the plants. Every important household received the news from their own foreman, who had seen the disaster earlier that morning. When the first rays of the sun pierced the sky, the coffee beans, still completely green—not the least bit darkened and with still a lot of growing to do—and the little shoots that announced the arrival of the cocoa pod all fell to the ground without the intervention of any hail shower or other kind of storm, without any rhyme or reason whatever. The tips of the branches of the cocoa and coffee plants looked stunted, as if the ends had been nipped off, and the green fruit, unripe and unusable, lay scattered on the ground. Nothing like this had ever happened before. There were lamentations in our houses that far surpassed any grief over the dead birds. It was a direct blow against our pockets, for the livelihoods of our townsfolk depended far more on the coffee, cocoa, and oranges of our plantations than on cattle.

In the afternoon white spores were blown across the town, so many of them floating in the air that the town seemed buried under a white mist. Our ceiling fans sent them dancing around the bedrooms and even seemed to attract them, creating whirlwinds of cotton balls that resisted any attempt to budge them. The corners of rooms and streets were cloaked with a woolly whiteness, like pillows fit for a princess. Then the pink light of sunset turned it into a fiery-colored fluff that we had to sweep hurriedly away, because it was starting to emit a penetrating stink of sulfur as the fluff turned into smoke. We ended up sweeping the whole town clean of the intolerable stink, waving our brushes around like fans. Luckily, our maneuver was successful and the stink was banished before we succumbed to vomiting and headaches.

10

The Earth Tremor

The following Sunday there was an earth tremor. I'm not saying we'd never had tremors before; we had, but never on a Sunday. We usually had them when we kids were in school, with the nun screaming in panic, "The end of the world has arrived!" But it all ended merely in our laughing mockingly at her. But this time the earth trembled as we were finishing off preening ourselves to go to church for the nine o'clock mass, the Indians having left the church by then and gone off to market their seeds. As if it wasn't upsetting enough for the earth to quake on a Sunday, the roof of the market also collapsed. And we all, children, women, adult males, spent the rest of the day rescuing the people who had been trapped under it.

Grandma didn't want to let me go and help. "They're just Indians there," she said. But she made the mistake of saying it in front of the priest, who turned on her, telling her that what she had just said was totally indefensible. "But they're a bunch of brainless idiots," she dared to reply. At that, he told her that she'd better not dare to say that again in his presence or in the presence of God anywhere, that the Indians were not one bit less human than she was, and that either she could let me go help them of her own free will or she'd have to answer for it in the

confessional. So I went off with the others and put myself at the
disposal of the secondary school teacher who had organized squads
of workers to raise the fallen pieces of cardboard and tangle of
sticks that had trapped the Indians. Under the collapsed roof they
were uttering loud, piteous complaints. One squad had the job
of helping them as they emerged, another gave them food and
drink, another had to patch up their wounds and calm them down
and usher them to one side so that they didn't impede the work
of the rescuers. As he gave them his blessing, the priest took advantage of the occasion to ask each of them if he'd been baptized. Those who answered no, he seated on a bench he'd had
brought from the church. When the bench was full, he had them
bring another. When this other was full, he himself went for the
third, ordering us not to let any Indian get away while he was
away. Benches weren't ordinarily used by the Indians at Masses;
benches were pushed aside against the walls, allowing the crowds
of Indians to mill around. So now, here in the open air, those
who had just escaped the ruins of the market sat on them with
exquisite propriety, as immobile as statues. Thus, when the priest
went for the third and then a fourth and then a fifth bench, not
one of the unbaptized Indians attempted to run off. However,
some of the Indians who had claimed that they'd already received
baptism pushed their way onto the already crowded benches. I'm
not sure whether they wanted a comfortable seat or whether they
were emotionally affected, like the rest of us, by the sight of their
companions formed into a solemn group, a frieze of ceremoni-
ous expectation. The majority were old men or women, of two
or three different ethnic groups. Some of the women were bare-
chested, while others were shrouded to the tops of their heads
in dark rebozos. Some wore skirts and blouses embroidered in
bright colors, while their neighbors were clad totally in white.

The whole Sunday was spent rescuing these buyers and
sellers of seeds. When night fell, we witnessed their collective

11

Grandmother's Story

"When we lived on the farm, the first day of each month, including January, even though it was a religious festival, we made a trip to visit an aunt who was sick both night and day. Her illness had left the skin of her body and her face marked with stripes. The spiteful people of the town called her 'the zebra from the Caribbean.' She lived quite near to our farmhouse, because she owned the adjacent farm to the south and had built her house at its northernmost limit in order to be close to us. But her decision had not paid off since we saw her only once a month. Getting to her place was a real expedition; it took us well over three hours of fast going to get there. The road that led from our farmhouse actually took us farther from hers, so we traveled instead along uneven tracks, and as we got closer to her house, even these disappeared. It was always the same man who guided us, using his machete to chop lianas and branches out of our way, slashing at them with the cold indifference of an animal treading on a daisy. The jungle was out to defy him, but not even an expert eye could have guessed the force he expended against it. Elegantly, like a butterfly floating on the breeze, he swung his machete, twisting his head so that his Panama hat danced on it, but his efforts left him bathed in sweat. His arms were deeply sunburnt, his muscles as hard as logs, the prominent veins looking as if they'd been carved there by a chisel. He'd leave our farm wearing a long-sleeved shirt, but midway on the journey, he'd roll up his sleeves, careless of the biting insects and the spiny thorns and the leaves that caused skin rashes, with no protection against the dengue fly or the terrible bite of the black widow, not worried that a scorpion might drop down on him from above and poison him with its deadly bite. When we reached our destination, he'd roll down his sleeves, put in his cuff links, and, despite being drenched in sweat, adopt the air of a gracious and imperturbable gentleman.

"On the way there he never once turned around to look at us or spoke a single word. My grandmother called him 'the German' and told us that as a boy he had gone around exposing pyramids in order to photograph them, but that after some contretemps, whose exact nature was never made clear, he'd decided he wanted no more of 'those absurd piles of stones.' Instead he lavished on the jungle a love that bordered on the fanatic, the kind of love, I imagined, he'd once lavished on the absurd piles of stones. With the same ease with which he swung the machete to left and right, mastering the most overgrown masses of growth, as if God had created him expressly for this purpose, he would sketch drawings of each one of the jungle plants on huge sheets of papers that he'd had sent especially from Europe. Then, he would color them in with a patient exactitude, writing down their names, and on a second sheet listing their qualities: smell, dimensions, type of blossom and fruit, etc. Then he'd move on to the next one, in what was a labor without end, with so many herbs, so many plants, so many trees, and so many flowers thronging our jungle.

"He was always impeccably dressed, as if on the point of leaving for a party. He had a room next to the house of my aunt's nurse, and my grandmother said he was the only consolation she had in the world. How did the German console an aunt who was sick both night and day? Well, I never even dared put the question into words.

"One first of September, when we had to sleep over at my aunt's place because a spectacular storm had broken, the German came into the kitchen in the evening and without saying a word got out an unbelievable number of eggs and beat them with a wild energy. He then put the same energy into frying up for us some inflated fritters, like hollow buns, which we ate with the milky juice you get from fig leaves. They were exquisite.

"I said to him, 'I really love your fritters, Mr. German. Thanks so much.'

"He replied, 'I'm not German. I'm Austrian.'

"'Well, where were you born?'

"'In the Vatican.'

"'Then you're not German or Austrian, either. And that's why you've never married. You were born in the land of priests and altar boys.'

"'My father was the agent of the Duke of Baden-Baden and managed his affairs in the Vatican. He spent three years there with his family. That's where I was born, and that's where we buried my mother, who died very young. I hadn't reached my second birthday before we were back in Baden-Baden. I don't have one memory of the Vatican. I was German, but I changed my nationality when I came to Mexico as a volunteer with the army of the emperor Maximilian. And here I stayed, looking after piles of stones and getting only insults for it, till I turned my eyes to the plants, and they're what occupy me now.'

"'The German isn't Austrian either,' said my grandmother. 'He's been here so long he's more Mexican than tamales and *mole*.'

"'What do you mean *mole*?' he replied. 'We don't eat that stuff around here.'

"'Did you really come with Maximilian? You must be really ancient,' I said with the astonishment to be expected of a child.

"My grandmother gave me a clout for being cheeky.

"'Let her alone,' he said. 'She's right and I'm not offended.'

"'Well, I am offended,' said my grandmother. 'You're younger than I am. And if I'm up to making these trips, I'm not having anybody calling me aged, just imagine, when we've traveled all that way through jungle, with all that heat, and all those ups and downs, any one of my bones could have gone snap, I don't know how they didn't . . .'

"The aunt who was sick both night and day had one key symptom—she couldn't distinguish dark from light. A strange infirmity made her insensitive to light. She saw everything in a misty light, though she hadn't cataracts or anything similar in her eyes; it was just something sick inside her that caused it. Since night and day were the same to her, she had trouble sleeping. She'd be wide awake or fast asleep regardless of the time of day. Sometimes she spent days in nightgowns that were embroidered to the point of looking ridiculous, and that night we spent stranded at her house I caught dreamy glimpses of her walking about the house, dressed like she was heading off to a fancy party, but the grandfather clock was striking four in the morning.

"She simply didn't have the same clock as other people, and there was no pretending she did. She had only one goal in life, and it got in the way of even the most basic forms of politeness—I mean to sleep. She dedicated herself to that goal with admirable tenacity, but, sadly, got very poor results. She was lucky if she got an hour of sleep. Usually it was no more than fifteen minutes at a time. Then she'd wander around for hours trying to nod off or get some sort of rest, stumbling around with her misty vision, or stretched out on her bed, her mind rambling.

"I felt very sorry for her. She suffered far too much with that horrible disease. They say she got it from an insect bite in the jungle. It must have happened when she was strolling there with the German . . ."

12

The Army

The following Sunday the army marched into town. Minutes before the clock struck eight, while the church bells were summoning the faithful to the second Mass of the day, there arrived in the park four trucks painted green from top to bottom. An uncounted number of uniformed men clambered down from them, armed to the teeth. The vehicles moved away and the men took control of the town center without giving a word of explanation to anyone. First they formed up to block all entrance to the porch of the church. The priest came out to see why he had only two parishioners inside, two old biddies who heard Mass after Mass, stuck like toadstools to the pews, and why the statues of the saints, the images of the Virgin Mary, the candlesticks, and the flower vases had all suddenly fallen out of their places over the altar's top, down from all its nooks and crannies. Fully dressed to say Mass in his vestments of white and gold, he collided with the army of green men, behind which he assumed his parishioners were waiting. Without changing his dress, he tried to pass through the wall of men, but each soldier was holding his rifle horizontally just below the level of his helmet and they formed an impenetrable barrier. He asked to speak with the general or the colonel or the ranking officer.

But nobody paid him any attention, as if they hadn't a clue what he meant by "general or colonel or ranking officer." For their reply they stared at him head-on, though in reality, since they were so focused on standing firm and holding their weapons just right, they barely saw him.

"What a screw-up!" the priest was thinking, he told us later. "Another Sunday without a Mass. What'll become of my flock?"

If it isn't disrespectful to the clergy, I imagine he was also saying: "What bloody bad luck! Things are really screwed up now. I'm not going to be able to fuck my little shepherdess in our hammock!"

To top it off, the poor priest had to suffer one more aggravation. In front of him the formation of soldiers—the hair under their gleaming helmets must have been smoldering in the heat of that tropical sun—blocked his way, but he was also unable to get through the side door of the sacristy because one of the trucks had now parked right against the wall, so he couldn't open the sacristy door. There he was stuck with the two old biddies, his altar boys, and his indefatigable nuns, unable to leave and eat breakfast, even though his guts were rumbling. At eleven-forty, according to the town clock on which we all relied—it was set on top of a column of carved wood, at the entrance of the furniture store on the corner of Hildalgo facing the park—the soldiers started to faint. Whose idea had it been to put metal helmets on their heads in this heat? It was absolutely insane. We never found out why in hell's name they'd come into town, though we suspected they'd heard about the problem with the market roof and that the central government had sent them, with its usual efficiency, to "help the victims," but that's only a guess, because nobody made clear what job they were expected to do. What nobody could doubt was that the sun had beaten them. The heat finished them off, knocking them over one after another.

No sooner had they collapsed than the priest, in absolute fury, dashed from the porch, without even looking at them, crossed the park, and marched off to his traditional Sunday breakfast, without one sign of sympathy for the fallen. We and the three nuns followed after him, treading on his heels, and the rest of the townsfolk followed his example, in that nobody was ready to help the victims of the sunstroke.

It was quite a while before the other soldiers, two in each vehicle, the driver and his mate, woke up from their midday nap and came down to the square to find their missing comrades. They went from house to house asking for water without the least sign of friendliness and then doused the fainted soldiers in bucketfuls.

On our return from breakfast the park was streaming with water. In the midst of the steam that the heat was creating, soldiers staggered about unsteadily, supported on the shoulders of the eight still-healthy men who bundled them like parcels into the trucks, which were also wrapped in fog. They took so long about it that by the time the last of the soldiers was aboard, there wasn't a trace of water left in the park or one soldier capable of standing to attention. The trucks made off, their springs squeaking. A few waterlogged weapons remained on the ground and the priest had them taken into the sacristy. Afterward, he told me to pass the word along that he'd be saying Mass at six o'clock. In the circumstances, Mass turned out to be straight speechifying. We gathered in the church and the priest harangued us with every sort of argument against the army, weapons, wars, preaching peace in a lengthy, moving sermon that took so long he could have said two High Masses in the time. When he saw his flock starting to snooze off, he glanced at the clock and promised to finish off the Mass the next Sunday. It goes without saying that there was no strolling through the park that day, with the men

13

The Electric Storm
and the Toads

As dawn broke the following Sunday, a truly memorable electric storm descended on us, one that had distressing consequences. The bandstand in the middle of the park was struck by lightning and burned up, as was the machine for making ice cream that had only just come to town. Lightning struck the giant kopak tree which overshadowed the bandstand, and the store below the bandstand, on the opposite side from the ice-cream store, was also reduced to ashes. Not even its display window survived, or a single item of merchandise. Even the canned goods were destroyed, but the benches outside the ice-cream store were left intact, as if the lightning had left them to the cruel mercies of sun and rain.

The entire town was astonished at this happening. To crown it all, we lost a cow. It arrived at our house, fried to a crisp, brought to us by four Indians who had loaded it on to a long pole in order to carry it. It was truly a sight for sore eyes, as black as coal and as shiny as the night sky. The Indians were insisting on bringing it into the house, but my grandmother said no, and as there was never any doubt about who ruled our household with a rod of iron, it stayed outside on the sidewalk. They'd hardly rested its four legs on the ground when it practically fell to ashes.

When the Indians picked up their pole, all that remained was a pile of blackness and a section of the head, still recognizable because one remaining eye kept staring at us. The crumbling of the cow was testified to by a mass of witnesses.

Grandma flew into a fury because "those good-for-nothings had come bringing that heap of filth." But the Indians did not respond to her scolding. They'd toted the frizzled cow all the way from the farm so that my grandmother wouldn't be able to accuse them of stealing it and have them thrashed, as usual. They hadn't been able to wake up the foreman, because the day before, he had celebrated his birthday, filling himself so full of rum that not even the electric storm or the calls of the Indians could rouse him from his drunken sleep.

The out-of-town bus arrived several hours late and we kids ran to see what had happened. The driver was pale and speechless. The passengers looked terrified. They sat on the benches in the waiting room and needed a glass of soda pop before they could answer our questions. "Hey, what happened to you guys? What took you so long? Why do you look like that?"

The oldest female passenger was the first to speak. "I've only ever seen one before, except that now with the awful noise of the bus . . ."

"When did you see it?" I asked, without the least clue what she was talking about.

"I suppose I was your age, little girl. It was a rainy afternoon. I was out riding with my papa, sitting in front of him. We were on our way back from—yes, I remember it well. How would I forget a thing like that? On our way back from my mother's funeral. Poor thing!" She crossed herself. "God bless her. We had taken her back to her town, and were returning to our own, when all of a sudden we saw it cross the road in front of us, coming on and on and on and on, till its tail disappeared across the other side of the road. Just like that it vanished into the thick bush. The horse didn't even whinny, Goldy was a fine creature, obeying my father's least order. All three of us remained motionless, looking at the giant serpent, so quiet it probably didn't realize we were there watching its endless length crossing and crossing and crossing in front of us. That's why it didn't devour us. But when you're in a noisy bus, how are you going to keep that quiet? There we were, making such a clatter, and then that happened!"

"This one today was unbelievable. I've heard folks say they're pretty immense, but this must have been all of forty feet!"

"You're kidding! It was at least fifty."

"No, even bigger than that!"

"It just didn't want to go. It stayed there, in front of us, rearing its horrible, snaky head."

"Of course, it had a snake's head, but what else would it have?"

"It coiled itself around, real bold-like, coiling along the road."

"We ought to have run over it."

"Right, sure! It would have wrapped itself around the bus and rolled it over and we'd have all got our heads smashed in."

The passengers had all started to talk at once, giving their different versions of the event, but however big the serpent had been, I lost interest and went back home.

They were still cleaning up the mess from the burnt cow. The ashes were greasy, and since it was Sunday our reliable Ofelia wasn't around. Grandma had managed to hire two girls from the town and they were busy scrubbing and scraping.

"If you want my opinion," I said to myself but in a voice loud enough to be heard, "that stain is here to stay."

"You don't know anything," said one of the girls, maybe younger than I was, raising her face to mine. "We've gotten rid of worse than this."

"Remember the time we cleaned that room at Alvarez's place?" her sister asked her in a conspiratorial tone. It had to be her sister, they looked so much alike. Then she looked at me and said, "They'd killed him with a machete. The whole place was full of blood and bits of brain—the floor, the walls, the windows, the mattress. We cleaned it up good, my sister and me did. Left it as clean as a new pin."

"Fit for a queen."

"It took us a few days, but with all that scrubbing and scrubbing, it came up like new."

"We threw out the mattress."

"Oh yeah, we threw out the mattress."

"We scrubbed it and scrubbed it but couldn't get the blood out, no way. I think they'd stuffed a dead man inside it, so no wonder we couldn't get the blood out. That's why we decided to throw it away."

"The trouble was this kid buried it behind the house."

"But the nice thing was that the place he buried it in grew lots and lotsa hydrangeas. You do know, dontcha, that hydrangeas feed on blood?"

"The awful thing was that the last days we were there cleaning, the dead man from inside the mattress appeared to us."

"He grabbed us by the feet and pulled."

"But we didn't quit cleaning, did we, not till the job was properly done."

"We used Fab soap powder. It was Fab here, Fab there, Fab everywhere."

I didn't contradict a thing they said, though I didn't believe a word of it. It was time to get dressed for our Sunday stroll. By now there was a threat of another storm. Mama was already dressed for strolling, but Grandma turned on her, saying it was a dumb idea to think of going for a stroll around an incinerated bandstand, I mean how dumb could you get, today of all days when no woman in her right mind would be venturing out to the park. And at that moment it started to rain, and how!

We made a dash for the living room of the house, as did the two girls who specialized in cleaning up blood. Dulce ran to her room, while old Luz stayed in the kitchen. Grandma quit arguing with Mama and started to tell her some story or other. The cleaning girls spoke to me in a low whisper, once again about being grabbed by the feet in the room at the Alvarez's house, when suddenly all the toads that the Almighty had created in this region of the globe started to jump up and hurl themselves against the windows of the part of the house that faced the river, against the walls, against whatever, and night fell without the rain ceasing nor the toads smashing themselves against the house. Now there were no streaks of lightning or rumbles of thunder, nothing to shed light on the atrocity of the toads, which was getting nastier, the darker it got.

On Monday I went to school at the usual time, overtired but punctual. All the students were talking about the behavior of the toads and nobody had any thought for the incinerated cow or the giant serpent, and the business of the bandstand came close to being taken for granted. All the talk was of the toads, wherever you went. On the patio one of the bigger girls said it was all the priest's fault, because he was up to all kinds of filthy tricks with the nuns. I was a lot smaller than she was, but that didn't stop me from arguing back. I told her it was a cheap lie from beginning to end, that Father Lima didn't do anything dirty with the nuns, that I knew what I was talking about, and that her teeth would fall out for being such a liar.

She said I was just a kid and what did I know? "You don't even know what filthy tricks are."

"It's a filthy trick when a man and a woman take off their clothes in a hammock and start making noises like pigs at the slaughterhouse and sucking and licking and pinching—"

All the girls started to laugh and I stopped my explanation. But they didn't talk badly of the nuns again and they decided to blame the electric storm and its aftereffects, the giant serpent and the carbonized cow, on the craze for chewing bubble gum that had swept through the school the previous week.

By the time school was over, we were all convinced of this and there wasn't a single student among us with bubble gum in her mouth. I felt curiously happy and victorious. The sisters had escaped the stain of calumny and the priest's reputation was intact thanks to my stunning intervention. How had I managed to fool them so easily? I kept asking myself. I was sure that none of them had any idea what filthy tricks were, any more than I did, but my version, because of its outlandishness, struck them as convincing. I had returned evil with good, I told myself. And for a while I felt positively angelic, a creature of sweetness and light. When I got home, I observed that the cleaning girls had received reinforcements. A virtual army was at work scraping windows and walls. It didn't consist of goofy girls but Indian women cleaners. I went down to the riverside and saw the same scene repeated at all the houses there. Where had they gotten so many Indians to do the cleaning? They'd brought them in from the farms, interrupting their work in the fields, at the cattle ranches, and on the coffee plantations. In the evening they came into the central patio to have supper out of an enormous cauldron of *pozole* which old Luz had specially made for them. It was one of the few nights that Grandma didn't tell her tales. She and Dulce came into my room and bolted the door, and Dulce combed her hair in silence, while out under the sky the barefoot Indians sang hymns to the Virgin Mary, before curling up to sleep on the ground.

Songs, laments, solemn howlings, filled with drawn-out notes and syllables, transmitted an ancestral grief, recalling ancient hardships, much more ancient than the Virgin herself, appealing to her from their need for shelter, for a naked, melancholy kindness, so plaintive and so goodly that it stirred one's fears.

When I awoke the next morning, there was no sign of the Indians. They had been taken away in trucks to their places of work, and those there was no room for had had to walk there. However, the Gypsy encampment had reappeared. On my way home from an errand, one of their women said to me, "Hey, you there, little girl."

It was strictly forbidden to talk to the Gypsies, because, according to Grandma, they stole little children, hiding them on hooks under their broad skirts and taking them away to beg in distant countries, sometimes poking out their eyes if they weren't pretty, and other times drugging them to sleep both day and night with their potions. And as well, they said, their women didn't have a shred of decency, while all the men were thieves.

"You know why that cow got burned up on your ranch?" the Gypsy woman asked me, boldly, staring me in the eyes, though I'd no idea who gave her the right to talk to me that way.

"Because it got struck by lightning," I replied with equal boldness.

"Come on! Don't be stup—" she said, swallowing the final syllable.

"I'm not stupid. Don't say I am. I saw it with my own eyes. Don't try to fool me."

"He got that way from eating mangoes."

"You're the one who's stupid, Gypsy. What's mangoes got to with being burned to a cinder?"

"It's very simple. Do you really think that mangoes are eaten the whole world over? That cow, who knows where they brought it from—"

"It was a fine zebu. It could put up with all sorts of weather. They come from India."

"I guarantee it comes from somewhere where they don't eat mangoes. It tried one, it liked it—well, who doesn't—then it had another, and then another, and then one more, till its guts caught fire, and in the end its flesh and its skin, till it was burned up from top to bottom, inside and outside. The same happens to blond little girls like you who eat too much from this country. Be careful, little girl, be careful. Do you want me to read your palm? Give me a coin and I'll read your future. Give me your hand. I know how to see into the future."

I gave the Gypsy my hand. She looked at it attentively. Then she closed it and said to me, looking into my eyes, "No, I can't read it for you. I don't like to take coins from the people who have your sort of luck. Don't eat any more mangoes. I figure that one half of your heart has already turned yellow, and the other half is turning brown with the heat, that's what I figure."

14

Old Luz

The following Sunday, when old Luz awoke, she was bearing the stigmata of Christ. As if this were a mere nothing, she sat down in her wooden chair to grind up the recently roasted coffee, but found she couldn't turn the handle of the mill because the wounds made by the nails prevented her, and she burst into tears. My grandmother found her crying and immediately sent for Dr. Camargo, who took one glance at her and sent for the priest. By this time Luz was levitating, her chair and all floating off the ground, and she kept insisting on clapping her hands so that she and I could sing together as usual, while my grandmother scolded her for all the blood she was splashing around the kitchen. In spite of her wounds and the harsh words, Luz's face wore a radiant smile. "Don't the wounds hurt?" I asked. Obviously they didn't, and that proved they weren't marks of illness but signs of Christ's blessing. Her blouse was soaked in blood.

The priest pulled at his hair when he realized that this was one more Sunday he'd have to spend without saying Mass and enjoying the pleasures of the hammock. "This had to go happen on a Sunday," he was saying to himself, but we caught his words. "This lovely miracle had to go happen on a goddam Sunday!" Old Luz felt a need to go pee and she landed her chair gently on the ground. Then with the help of my nanny, Dulce, she directed her feeble, faltering steps to the bathroom. She was longer in there than usual. She wasn't coming out or answering our calls. When Dulce forced the door of the tiny windowless cubicle to see what was happening, she discovered that Luz wasn't there. At the foot of the toilet bowl rested the old lady's clothing, her shoes, her long gray skirt, the blouse, the underskirt, the knickers, and the blood stains that had drenched the shoes. That was all. Our dark-skinned Luz had dissolved in urine. But Dulce wasn't giving up the search and called on everybody, the priest, the doctor, my grandmother, my mother, the three nuns, and even the neighbors, to help find the missing woman. They all peered into the cubicle, without any idea of what was going on, and saw there the clothing and the toilet bowl containing pee. Grandma and the doctor inspected it carefully, while the three nuns sang a dog-Latin hymn in praise of Jesus. The priest was muttering prayers, while the neighbors dashed out to spread the news around town. Old Luz couldn't have concealed herself in a nook or cranny of the cubicle, because there weren't any. It was impossible to believe that she had slipped away unnoticed from the cubicle. So they pulled the chain, gathered up her clothes, and the priest sent a message to ring the church bells to announce her death. While the bells pealed out, he headed off to the church, eager to say Mass. It had already struck nine o'clock and the church was packed with both Indian and white parishioners, on this rare occasion mixed together, for they'd been waiting there for two hours in the midst of all sorts of rumors, some of which included Luz and some of which didn't. From the pulpit the priest explained how Luz had met her end, and how she had passed away in an odor of sanctity, omitting that it was an odor strongly tinged with urine.

Thanks, maybe, to the blessed sign shown us by the saintly old Luz, and to something else that happened during the week but escaped my girlish eyes, the priest was obliged to make a decision. He came to the house to tell us about it that Thursday evening: henceforth he would be spending Sunday in Agustini. Neither the priest nor Mama nor I ever returned to the old routine. The priest opted to break up his Masses over three days; Sunday, he would stay in the parish; Fridays and Saturdays he would come and go, extending the area of his preaching. On Fridays Mama would go with him. For his trips on Saturdays—which was house-cleaning day, so Grandma wouldn't have let her go—he didn't even ask for her company. He just said that on that day he'd be traveling alone, off to God knows how many settlements.

15

God Rested

On the following Sunday, the tenth of this bizarre set, the God of our town, unfaithful to the tradition that the number seven should be the one for rest, finally relaxed. He allowed our morning routines to resume their usual pattern, as if all He had been waiting for in order to switch off his machinery of raging monstrosities was the decision of the priest not to travel with me on Sundays. Grandma, Mama, and I accepted this decision, without one unsaintly grumble.

Funeral Masses were said for the soul of old Luz, who had spontaneously turned into Doña Luz. At the Indian Mass they filled the nave of the church with flowers, songs, dances, and a fragrant incense, which had not dispersed even by the time the altar boys were setting up the benches for the nine o'clock Mass which we attended, clad, without exception, in lugubrious black. In the vestibule the Indians had left a lovely carpet made of flowers and seeds of various colors. Inside, the nave was full of candles and branches of orange-colored cempasuchil, laid at the foot of the walls and pillars. The lingering perfume also helped to make the ceremony profoundly moving. I spent the mass weeping for my little old lady, remembering her caramels, her hand clapping, her flan, her way of slaughtering hens and turtles, her songs, and the babies howling away feebly. Dulce wept inconsolably, and when the rest of us left, she remained behind on her bench, motionless in her grief.

We left her there to cry to her heart's content and walked on to the priest's house. After breakfast, at which the nuns, also dressed in mourning, went back to discussing the embroidery of the tablecloth, with a concentration and energy worthy of a Vatican Council, we seated ourselves on the benches and hammocks in the garden, on the opposite side from the laurels and the flowering shrubs that the nuns fussed over, near where the river slid by. Chatting aimlessly, we watched the water gliding away and the boats of the fishermen bobbing gently. Grandma too sat with us, instead of rushing home as she usually did. She listened to the chatter of the nuns, the priest, Mama, and me without interrupting. She didn't utter a peep, till suddenly she said, "Well, you see . . ."

16

Grandmother's Story

"You have to realize that this territory was once governed by a man who hadn't been born here but in Cuba, in the days when it was simpler to go to Havana and back than it was to go to Villahermosa. Back then there were no ferryboats to cross the rivers. You had to leave your horse on one side of the River Tancochapan and get another mount on the other side, and the same again at the Mezcalapa, not to mention the Grijalva and the Usumancinta, two vast bodies of water you had to cross to reach the capital, which in those days wasn't even called Villahermosa but St. John the Baptist. I won't touch on going to Mexico City. It was out of the question, since there weren't any roads to get there.

"This man, Francisco Sentmanat, married one of the sisters of my grandmother, the eldest one, to be precise. Poor thing, what a life she had to lead! It was a love match, not a marriage of convenience, though by the time they did marry, more than one person assumed it was ambition that was leading her down the aisle, because at that period Sentmanat was the owner of Tabasco. Nobody said no to him; he always had the last word on everything. I think that he had genuine feelings for my aunt Dorita. Otherwise, how can you explain it, eh? He had his pick of so many girls, so why was he going to tie himself to a girl who was less wealthy than he was and who, they say, wasn't really all that pretty. I don't say she was ugly, because none of my mother's sisters was ugly, but Dorita, well, there's no denying it, she was the least gifted, shall we say, people didn't rave about her eyes the way they did about Sara's or about the china-doll complexion my grandmother had, or about the hourglass waist of little Nena . . .

"Anyway, it turns out that this Sentmanat did just what he pleased till his excesses exhausted everybody's patience and they threw him out of Tabasco. He was a tyrant, there's no denying it. I have to admit it, even though we're related. On the good side he declared the independence of Tabasco, saying that this was what we needed, and why not? But on the bad side, he was a cheap and nasty sort, forever pulling a fast one wherever he could, though where he thought he got the right to do so, I can't say, but he was full of caprices and ambitions and because of his character he had people assassinated for no real reason or stuck in jail, regardless of who they were. As well, even though he was genuinely fond of Aunt Dorita, he grabbed any woman he fancied, as if all the women in Tabasco were Indians and he could have a tumble with them in a cane field or coffee plantation and never face the consequences. He raised taxes outrageously, transferred other people's property into his name, whether it was an established farm or not. Oh, his government became intolerable, so bad that even our family, the Ulloas, who were related to him, turned against him. Ages before, the government in Mexico City had declared his position illegal, but what the devil did he care? Back then, they were so far away, as I said. It would have been more to the point if Havana or Mérida had declared war on us, but that didn't happen. Sentmanat was the close friend of the governor of the Yucatán and did an incredible amount of business with the Cubans and the Spaniards in Cuba. But the upshot was that the Ulloas and the other Tabasco families finally kicked him out, because without help from anybody, he'd earned his expulsion, thanks to all his wild ways and crazy messes there's no point in even mentioning.

"He went off to live in New Orleans, with my poor aunt Dorita and all. They say he had a very nice house there. In fact they built three like it in St. John the Baptist, one of them belonging to my aunt Nena, Dorita's sister. Her husband had made it his personal business to get rid of Sentmanat as governor, and it wasn't as if Aunt Nena's husband was especially envious or liked to pick a fight, but Sentmanat brought it upon himself. Not content with being the big boss over everything in Tabasco, and with always having the last word in everything, and with being the representative of law and order, he declared the family's properties solely his own, and, worse still, confiscated land from people who weren't even related to him, if there was a single rubber tree growing on it. He was friendly with some Germans who had come to collect rubber, when they'd scented there were going to be big profits in it, because back in Europe they were using it to make all sorts of things like combs, shoes, billiard balls, buttons, buckets, electrical insulators, boxes, knife handles, and such. Sentmanat did the arithmetic and figured out there was a fortune in rubber, so he confiscated any property where rubber trees grew.

"Anyway, he did go off to New Orleans and he built a fabulous house there. And we all thought that we'd seen the last of him in Tabasco. But we'd underestimated him. The fact that the whole of Tabasco had turned against him didn't crush his spirit at all. So believe it or not, he organized a pirate expedition. On the Mississippi he fitted out two ships with guns and sailed across the Gulf of Mexico and came in via Paraíso, where he joined up with his German allies and reached St. John the Baptist and captured it in a surprise attack! It wasn't that he was a strategic genius.

He was just impulsive and whimsical. He never thought twice before doing anything. His blood was constantly on the boil, his brain worked overtime, but to think a thing over, to plan an act intelligently—that simply went against his grain. His victory was short-lived. I mean, he caught us off guard, because while he was away in New Orleans building his house and arming his pirate ships, we'd been decimated by an epidemic of yellow fever, a terrible business, really horrible to get, with lots of people dying, but even so, how could the state capital remain in the hands of pirates? At the start, you were just feverish, you know, it was like a mild cold with stomachaches thrown in, and an awful stuffiness, but then if it didn't go away, you got really sick, with your eyes all bright and unable to bear the light, and if it went beyond that, you were in for the worst of all endings, because you'd get an anxiety attack, then start vomiting up black stuff, as black as coffee grounds, and get delirious. It didn't matter how much morphine you took to stop the stomach pains or how many preparations of adrenaline you used to control the bleeding, there was nothing that worked to stop the convulsions or the hemorrhaging. Death was inevitable. They say that the corpses—well, so my uncle Juan told me, he was studying to be a doctor at the time—they had lesions in the duodenum and ulcerations in the heart. If they looked bad on the outside, they were even worse on the inside.

"So, because the epidemic of yellow fever had cut a swath through young and old, sparing only the very old and the very young, it was left to the kids to take up arms against Sentmanat. It was an army of youngsters who beat him and dragged him away to have him shot at Talpa without waiting around for any sort of trial. He arrived there with his body in shreds because they had literally dragged him there, like a load on a rope, bouncing around, more dead than alive, so they had to shoot him lying down, as there was no way they could keep him on his feet. They say that they considered tying him to a cross but immediately rejected the idea because it was a sort of blasphemy with his being an out-and-out rascal and the cross recalling memories of Christ. When a letter arrived at St. John the Baptist from Mr. MacIntosh—the man who came up with the idea of spreading rubber between two layers of cloth, the millionaire inventor of waterproof raincoats—he also had factories for making rubber sponges and was a buddy of Sentmanat in various enterprises and a personal friend of presidents and one of the richest men in the world—anyway, when his letter arrived, begging clemency for Sentmanat, it was too late. The deadly deed had been done. They say that once all the hullabaloo over Sentmanat's death had died down, the sisters of my grandmother and my aunt Dorita sailed off in the same schooners that had brought the pirates and headed for New Orleans, going straight to my aunt's house, and there they looted it, each one of them carrying off whatever she fancied, dresses, furniture, jewelry, paintings or sculptures, while Dorita wept buckets and asked them for mercy, reminding them that she was their sister, and Sara answered, 'Whose sister? If you didn't have the guts to stand up for my kids when your husband was leaving them without a square yard of land to their name, I don't know whose sister you reckon you are, you're certainly not mine. I've only come to collect what belongs to me, what you and your husband stole from my lands in his business deals with the Germans. This stuff is what you bought with the cakes of rubber your husband and his cronies went to sell in Europe in those English ships.'

"Then they sailed home with the schooners loaded with treasures. That's where we got that Ming dynasty vase in the living room, along with the other bits and pieces, though my grandmother didn't go to New Orleans, she was too young at the time, but her sisters saved her share of the booty, because all the Ulloa girls had this marvelous sense of right and wrong. And I think that includes even Dorita, in her way.

"Nobody knows what happened to the poor creature after that. I've heard it said that she turned into a loose woman, but really I don't believe it, for me that was all vicious gossip, because she was an Ulloa after all, so how can they think she'd get involved in that sort of thing, I mean, she wasn't born in the street, without a family name, without pride, without a mother and father. She'd had enough to put up with, losing that husband of hers, well, more than enough, considering the way he died, and after losing the affection, the love, the respect of her family, well, she was in no mood to go and live it up then, was she?

"Still, they do say that she went sailing up and down the Mississippi in the little boat she and Sentmanat had left Tabasco in, when we couldn't take any more of his excesses, selling her favors to all and sundry, and recruiting girls for that line of business, and that she made so much money at it that the marvelous house she'd had in New Orleans couldn't even compare with the one she had built in Baton Rouge, and that, fat and elderly, she now made out she was French, her pockets crammed with currency worth a lot more than the obsolete bills my uncles had piled up only to find they were good for nothing but heating the bread oven, because they had trunks jammed with banknotes that lost value overnight. This country is a disaster, I tell you, a total disaster . . ."

17

The Beach

The Thursday of the following week was a holiday, and Mama had the bright idea to take all three of us to the beach. She borrowed the priest's car, which he'd taught her to drive. It was the first time we'd seen her drive, but she did it with a manly aplomb we'd never have imagined of her. She wore a lovely white cotton dress enlivened with embroidery, with a sky-blue belt around her waist, possibly a bit out of style, but it made her look very youthful. She put on for the first time some dark glasses—"to see the road better"—and these took away any suspicion of looking old-fashioned. She was wearing a pale pink lipstick, with a slight sheen to it, the same color as her nails, which were always maintained in impeccable condition by the adoring girls at the beauty salon. "Your mom is such a lady, so fine . . ." About her neck she had a flimsy white, almost transparent, scarf. Grandma wore a short-sleeved blouse over a white skirt with dark markings and buttons down the front. They both put on wide-brimmed hats, Mama's white, Grandma's gray.

We traveled the usual road out of town, but then turned off toward Villahermosa. The road surface looked perfect to me, and though there were only two lanes, I thought it was a spacious and modern highway we were speeding down, almost flying. Grandma, who shared my opinion, complained about the speed, and I, all tense with my mouth wide open, was thankful that she did. To our right we saw the first of a whole line of gleaming dunes, almost golden in color, alternating with plantations of papayas, bananas, and coconuts, all so methodically laid out by human ingenuity and Mother Nature that it seemed reality itself till we collided with a mental bump against the true, ragged reality of the sea front. There chicozapote was growing in the middle of the great branches of enormous trees, a hard gemlike stuff sprouting out of the tender leaf tips, like a violent aberration in the center of the clustering growth. So many mangoes hung from the crowded trees that here and there they lent the foliage a yellowish tint. The giant kapoks were home to innumerable orchids and creepers, small universes of variegated greens. In trees along the edge of the highway, monkeys swung in hordes, and there was one moment when a flock of flamingos followed our car, cackling above our heads.

We passed a town called Tamarindo, a wretched place that owed its existence solely to the presence of the highway, a clutter of stalls, probably assembled on the spur of the moment solely for the purpose of selling motorists food and refreshments. There wasn't one tamarind tree to be seen on the town's single street; only people eating crab legs and long slices of fried banana, and drinking fresh pineapple juice. We drove through Paseo de Varas and Chalchihuacan, more serious settlements, with their colonial church and central park where youngsters could stroll in search of love and somebody to start a family with.

Finally we reached the sea. The first things we found were seafood restaurants with rowdy musicians, located in thatched huts with a cement floor and metal tables without a tablecloth that some beer factory had lent them in return for advertising their products. My grandmother's comment was "I for one have no intention of eating in those pigsties."

"Don't worry, Mama. I wasn't going to take you there for a meal. I've got something else planned."

The sand was fine and clean, the sea dark blue. As it was a holiday, there was a mob of people playing on the shore, kids, moms, grandmothers. There were lots of big fat mamas in nylon slips that the crashing waves had left transparent, revealing their gigantic flabby breasts, like secondary bodies viciously glued onto them, some with extraordinarily big bellies and thighs that had grown way out of control, at least according to my girlish criteria. These seal-like women looked gloriously happy, kids were howling with glee as they rolled around on the sand, mothers looked on smiling, fathers lying facedown on the sand let it infiltrate their underwear without moving a muscle. To be in the presence of the sea filled them all with exuberant joy, as if they were at the best of all possible parties. My grandmother observed them all with contempt from the thatched hut where we had been seated by two attentive boys. We were sipping fresh coconut milk.

"How they dare swim in those getups is beyond me," said Grandma. "God made bathing suits for that sort of thing. Stupid people who just don't know how to live!"

"But Mama, how can you say that? Bathing suits are really expensive."

"Then they oughtn't to go swimming."

A little boy in his underpants picked up a used straw from the sand and improvising a blowpipe out of it scored a well-deserved hit on Grandma with a screwed-up paper bullet. He hadn't heard what she'd said, but his intuition had told him she merited the aggression. Grandma didn't feel the paper land on her hair, but I glared at the kid with blazing eyes, fearing the worst if Grandma were to realize. Almost bursting with giggles, the little boy darted away.

"I don't know what's the matter with you, always sticking up for those deadbeats, they don't need your help, they can stand up well enough for themselves. They're what's wrong with this country, but you still—"

To avoid listening to them squabble, I got up from my chair, took off my dress, and ran in my bathing suit down to the sea. I left the deadbeats on the shore, rolling around with their sand-covered parents, and passing the women who looked like sea cows I swam off with the grace of a mermaid, while Grandma and Mama shouted for me to come back. For once I mattered. I kept on swimming till I reached the second beach, some three hundred yards out from them. I could still see them signaling with their arms for me to return. In view of all the energy they were putting into it, I realized I'd no option but to go back. The beach under my feet was covered in shells and starfish, though why we call them starfish when they're basically round, I don't know. I planned to return in a while to collect some. I didn't know what could have gotten into those two to make them shout so much, but I dived back into the water and swam back the way I'd come. When I got there, I stepped out of the water, taking large strides to join them quickly because they were still calling out at me to hurry up, their faces all twisted, shouting themselves hoarse.

With water dripping off me, I realized that they weren't the only two hysterics around; others were watching my arrival with concern. I turned my face to the horizon. Over the whole sea was stretched a second watery mantle, an enormous sheet of a lighter color, that in front of my eyes proceeded to gobble up the beach I had just visited.

"Silly girl!" Grandma was telling me. "How reckless can you get! You could have drowned. I mean, who'd get the crazy idea to swim so far off? It simply defies belief."

If you couldn't go in it, what was the sea for? I detached myself from the two nagging shrews. I heard people saying that it often happened, that this illusory beach would disappear as fast as it appeared, that you couldn't trust it, because the sea's second mantle would cloak the surface and drown anybody caught on the sandbar. The water had swallowed so many already; there was no counting the victims. I told as many as were willing to listen that I'd seen that beach covered in beautiful colored shells, with starfish and sea urchins.

A dark-complexioned girl of my age laughed at my words. "What's the big deal there, blondie?" she said. "What do you think is under the sea? Shells that aren't worth anything. You gonna sit down and make necklaces out of them like the Indians and sell them to gringos to hang around their necks?"

We had lunch at a restaurant with white tablecloths a little farther along. One of Mama's cousins was expecting us, an idiot who kept saying he wanted to marry her. Mama kept him as a kind of informal boyfriend, perhaps, I think now, to divert suspicion from her affair with the priest. But what was the cousin trying to hide? I never found out, yet there was something in his look that sent shivers up my spine. But I knew the history of his brother, as did the whole town. He was a pilot, he had a beautiful wife he beat up from time to time, he had six children by her, my cousins, blond Gypsies forever traveling from pillar to post, from their grandmother's house to their father's house, because intermittently there'd be a bust-up and the mother would leave her husband, but she always went back to him. He had her tied to him by the chilling magic of his family.

On our way home the priest's car crushed under its tires the crabs that were scurrying across the highway.

"This is the time crabs get massacred, daughter, on their way back down to the sea."

We kept on crushing them to bits with our car. On the beaches near Agustini everything was devoted to devouring and killing.

18

My Uncle and the Bakery

The town's bakery produced loaves of bread decorated in showy colors, doughnuts in strident Mexican pink, pancakes in royal blue, biscuits in lemon yellow. They even adorned their salty buns with a silly curlicue of colored sugar. For that reason, said Grandma, we never bought their individual items. She had them make large loaves for her without either coloring or sweetening, in place of those "disgusting monstrosities of the Indians." From Monday to Saturday our bread was ready just before lunch, so we always ate it freshly baked. On Sundays Grandma made toast from the week's leftovers, and anything else that remained, supposing that something did remain, went into a bread pudding with raisins and a glass of rum, along with almonds and slices of other nuts. It was an exquisite dessert.

Our household, like all the households of the better class of people, ate only white bread, but there were minor differences. The bread in the Juarez home was a little more voluminous than ours, and being a large family, they ate not one loaf a day but two. The loaves of the nuns were the same size as ours but had a cross set in the crust, made out of the same dough as the bread, and it was delivered in half dozens every other day. The Ruizes didn't like big loaves. For them the bakery made round loaves that they called "country bread." According to my grandmother, it was obvious they were still uncooked in the center and she claimed that it was eating raw dough that had given their youngest child, Ivan, his convulsions. The doctor had demolished her theory on numerous occasions, but she persisted in her belief and continued to preach it. She wouldn't quit till she had convinced the whole town, the Ruizes included, that the round loaves were dangerous.

The doctor's family preferred little loaves, almost the size of the buns with the sugared curlicue. The Vertizes, like the Ruizes, didn't like loaves at all. For them they baked bread in the same shape as the buns with curlicues of sugar, but with two sharp points and the same size as our loaves.

All these special orders were set out on trays at the bakery, but with their destination unspecified. There was never any mix-up; nobody ever took somebody else's bread. Each family came by every day for its own order, and if they needed more they put in a request the previous evening.

Early one Sunday morning the phone rang. It was my uncle Gustavo. He told my grandmother that he would be coming to lunch that day. Grandma repeated everything he said, so that Dulce and I could know what he was telling her. He was bringing along his fiancée and her brother-in-law, to introduce them to us. China Jack, whom we'd met the previous year, was also coming. My uncle then asked Grandma to put me on the line.

"Delmira, my favorite niece, how are you?"

"Stop clowning, Uncle Gustavo. I'm your only niece."

"That's why you're my favorite, my favorite little chick. I've a present for you and I'm bringing it over today. I can't wait to give it to you. Want to see it?"

"Yes!"

"There! What does it look like?"

"How do I know?"

"What do you think it is?"

"A Barbie!"

"I'm not going to tell you. It's a surprise."

"Tell me!"

"It's a surprise."

"Hey, Gus, what are you doing awake so early?"

There was a burst of laughter at the other end of the phone. I remembered clearly that when he lived with us, before I started school, he used to wake up later than I did.

"I got up early because I can't wait to bring you your present. Make yourself look pretty. I'm going to introduce you to a girl who—well, you never know, I could end up marrying. What do you think of that?"

"I think it's horrible. You promised me you wouldn't get married till after I did."

"And who's to say you won't get married first?"

"I say so!"

There was more laughter.

"I'll tell you a secret, but don't breathe a word of it to anybody, Delmira. Your uncle Gus is a confirmed bachelor, a hopeless case where marriage is concerned. This girl I'm bringing today has some crazy idea of trapping your handsome uncle into marriage, but she's not going to pull it off. I don't want to be the bad guy, so I'm bringing her over so she can enjoy your grandmother's cooking. She'll eat like a queen. When she realizes I was pulling her leg, that I went out with her just to have somebody pretty to dance with and show off on my arm, she won't be able to hate me, because at the bottom of her heart she'll be grateful unto death for your grandma's banquet. What do you say to that?"

"Sounds fine to me."

"See you in a while."

"Where are you?"

"In crummy old Villahermosa."

"That's quite a ways away."

"Come on! You could have said that yesterday. We got here late last night from Mexico City after driving all day. Now we're only six hours away. Ciao, bambina!"

He hung up. The household had already started up a whirl of activities in preparation for his visit. There would be no morning stroll for Dulce and me, even though it was Sunday. Grandma was sending her out to recruit more help.

"Bring back two of the cleanest girls you can find. Check out if Doña Luz's niece, Chole, is still around. Tell her to come and help me. But fancy Gustavo deciding to come and visit on a Sunday! And without proper notice. Oh, the bread!" she shouted, and then added, "Oh my God, the bread! Hey, Delmira, run and order the bread. Make sure they listen to you. Order four big loaves. It doesn't matter if it's too much. Get going over there right now. And don't come back without it. Go on, move it!"

The bells for seven o'clock Mass hadn't started chiming yet. Mama was still fast asleep; it must have been around six-thirty. Grandma had already changed her slippers for some outdoor shoes and was carrying shopping bags in her hand.

"Get dressed and run over to the bakery, girl! If you have to pay extra for them, just pay it and don't argue."

She took off at speed, but I took my own time in going back to my bedroom. Without closing the door, I pulled my nightgown off over my head and then quickly wrapped my dress around me. Dulce had just finished fixing my hair, so I wouldn't be going out disheveled. I washed my face and then heard Mama dragging her washbasin across the floor. I went to peep. Her door was shut, but in my imagination I saw her clearly just as if I were watching her—splashing water on her body in the way I've described to you and trying to catch it on her thighs and scoop it back up to retrace its path. I thought she would have the balcony door open and I was embarrassed to leave the house, but I recalled Grandma's urgency and, indifferent to embarrassment, I stepped out into the street. The balcony door was shut. I breathed deeply. Firmly shut.

Without dawdling along the way, I soon got to the bakery. It still wasn't open. I went around the side and knocked on the door there. Nobody answered. "Well," I thought, "then I might as well go in." I knocked on the door and I got the feeling that it wasn't bolted, only shut to. It was a tiny door, sized for dwarves. So I went in, plunging into the semi-gloom. Luckily I halted, because one step ahead of me lay a sharp drop and a narrow stairway.

"You nearly had a nasty fall there," I said aloud to myself. Then I added in a bold, singsong voice, "Hey-hey, halloooo! Anybody there?"

Nobody heard me. I listened to some noises coming up from below, something like a murmured conversation, but I couldn't see anything beyond the first steps of the stairway. I went down, calling out to see if anybody would hear me before I got to the bottom. But still no answer. The basement was faintly lit by small, high windows, protected by bars, that gave onto the sidewalk. In front of the stairs was a sloping ramp that ended in another opening, considerably narrower than the tiny door upstairs. It led to a patio and a brick oven where the bread was baked. Through it poured a stream of heat and light. Off to the right everything was smothered in a cloud of dust.

Once again I called out. "My grandmother sent me to order four loaves of bread for today."

"Who's there?"

"Delmira. Delmira Ulloa."

"How big do you want the loaves?"

I followed my ears toward the voice, since my eyes could not penetrate the cloud of flour, but once I'd entered the cloud things became apparent. The flour reflected the meager light of the basement like little mirrors, multiplying it. There, inside the cloud, everything was visible, although it seemed to be in slow motion and totally intangible.

I waved my hand in front of my face, but clearing some dust from my line of vision only returned me momentarily to the blinding darkness, until the cloud came back to my aid and suddenly I could see again. The fat man who'd asked me the questions was neither white nor Indian. His only ethnicity was flour. He was the first man of flour I'd ever seen. He was totally naked except for his white cotton underpants and an enormous handkerchief around his head, knotted behind, like the pirates illustrated in my books.

"Hey, you!" I said familiarly, because I wasn't sure how to address him. "I don't know how big the loaves should be. We pay two pesos a week for them."

"I'm not talking about the price. I'm talking about the weight. What weight do you want?"

"About this size," I replied, showing him with my hands the exact size I wanted.

"Tell me the weight and I'll make them for you. Otherwise, forget it."

Beside him, an equally fat man, reclining on the floor, was kneading with his feet an enormous ball of dough on a huge tray. It wobbled around, swaying backward and forward, like something alive.

A little beyond him a third man, skinny but dressed like the other two and of the same color, was shaping the dough into loaves on another huge tray. Everything there was white too. God knows how the bread got its fancy colors into it.

"But I don't know how much they weigh."

"You don't know, you don't get the loaves. As simple as that."

Then I had an inspiration.

"You know the loaves for the nuns, the ones with the cross on top? Make me four of those."

"With crosses as well?"

"No. Put a G for Gustavo on them."

"What's a G? I don't know my alphabet."

The floor was as pure white as driven snow. I crouched down and traced a capital G.

"Four loaves?" he asked.

"Right. Four."

"Four loaves coming up, blondie, in time for lunch. I'll get them ready right now and put that snake-thing on top, all curly. Or rearing, you said."

"Psst, pssst! Got anything to lend me, dearie?" shouted another man who was kneading with virile energy a thick welter of dough that had a yellowish tinge to it. He was doing it with his arms, chest, and one thigh completely sunk in the dough. For some reason I was reminded of the curate jammed up against my mother's buttocks. There was a striking similarity between the two things. I was so overcome with shame I hadn't the presence of mind to answer the man or even ask what he wanted me to lend him. I said a timid thank-you to the other fellow and took off fast. I shot up the stairs as if the men were chasing me.

When I got out to the street, I realized how appalling the heat had been down in that basement. In comparison the air up above was cool. The light too was so radically different from that down below that it was hard to believe it belonged to the same world. I rubbed my eyes and took a deep breath before starting my walk home.

On my way through the market I bumped into Grandma. Behind her toddled two boys laden down with shopping bags filled to the brim. One of them also carried an outsized hen, dead and featherless. Normally we never bought them in that condition. Doña Luz used to kill and pluck them herself, but now there was no Doña Luz and today we were in a hurry. The boy had fastened it with string around his waist in order to leave his hands free. He wasn't even as tall as I was. The hen's head bumped against his shins with every step he took. He smiled at me without embarrassment. His teeth were completely brown, like half-chewed caramels. His feet were bare. The other boy was taller than us, had his hair clipped down to his scalp, and also had a burden secured around his waist, a bunch of beetroots.

"What's that, Grandma?"

"Sugar beets."

"But you never buy them."

"Well, I did today. Get a move on. Don't block my way."

"I put in the order for the bread, Grandma. I asked them to put a G where they put a cross for the nuns."

"Can't you do anything right? Even when you get explicit instructions?"

I didn't bother to explain why I'd been driven to make the order this way. If she didn't like it, she could lump it. I was sure that Uncle Gustavo would love the G's, and that was what counted. She could get as nasty with me as she liked. Instead of answering her, I started to joke around with the boys.

"You've got teeth made of gold, right?" I said to the kid with rotten teeth.

The two boys laughed. Then I tried again. "Is that hen tickling your belly with its claws?" But Grandma grabbed me by the ear and said into it, "You don't talk to Indians. Have you got that? Okay?" And she gave me a sharp pinch.

We walked on to the house without a further word. Then she, Mama, and I went to hear Mass. But Grandma didn't join us for breakfast with the priest. She had to busy herself with the preparations for lunch. She invited the priest to drop in and eat with us, and he accepted gladly.

We walked over to the doctor's house and invited him as well. The rest of his family had gone off to Mexico City because somebody was marrying somebody there, and he too accepted gladly.

From there we hurried off to buy flowers, purplish gladioli with long stems, and back in the house we arranged them very prettily.

Mama slipped some worn table mats under the flower vases. The vases seemed to float, as usual, about a finger's breadth above the furniture, but they didn't chime in the wind the way Grandma's collection of bells did, responding to its gusts and even to the footsteps of anybody going by. If the living room was open because it was Saturday, the day for general cleaning, I used to jump up and down in front of the bells till their clappers tinkled. But on the rare occasions that we were entertaining people from out of town, the flower vases, the bells, and the porcelain Lladro figurines were placed on top of the furniture. Even the Virgin from the altar at the doorway came in and set her sacred feet in the wall niche.

In some other houses in town the sculpted figures insisted on lying flat, snuggling down, as if tired out by the endless heat. At the priest's place, the piggy bank on the windowsill above the kitchen sink was always tilted, with its front feet down the sloping ledge and its back feet raised. Our church gave us the feeling of a solar plexus in the process of breathing. All the images and the candlesticks rocked back and forth.

If invading forces had wanted to capture us by surprise, they never would have succeeded. Inside our houses we would have felt them the moment they set their first treacherous foot on our soil; the force of their arrival would have been transmitted to our ornaments and religious statues.

Once we'd organized the flower vases, we laid the table, putting on it a crocheted tablecloth made by Grandma, her wedding crockery, the silver cutlery, and the cut-glass wineglasses. We'd barely got the napkins in place when we heard Uncle Gus's car arriving. Now he was driving a fabulous, flaming-red Mustang, a model never before seen in Agustini, but God knows how it had survived all the potholes on the highway. He also had a camera with him and had us all come out for a photo.

"This is before I introduce anybody to anybody," he said, arranging where we should stand. "A photo of total strangers."

Just as he was about to take it, he asked, "Where's Doña Luz? I can't take a photo without her. Get her out here."

"Well, that's just not going to be possible," said Grandma. "Go ahead. Take the photo."

He didn't ask us to say "cheese," to get us all smiling, but just snapped us. I've still got that photo, I brought it to Germany with me. Behind us you can see kids milling around, their bellies on display, and youngsters from the town intrigued by the car and indifferent to us.

"What about Doña Luz, Mama?" asked Gus.

"She left us, son. Two weeks ago, she passed on to a better life."

"How come you never told me? I'd have come to the funeral."

"There wasn't a funeral," I interrupted.

His sad features registered astonishment.

"What did you say? No funeral?" he asked in slow, deliberate tones. "Why was there no funeral?" he added even slower. "She was one of the family, Mama. If it was a matter of money, you'd only to ask."

"What are you talking about?" said Grandma. "That wasn't the reason. In this town not even the most miserable wretch goes to a better life without flowers, a coffin, and tamales."

"She turned completely into pee," I interrupted again.

Gus looked at me with a smile all over his face.

Grandma glowered furiously. "That kid! I can't put up with any more from her!"

"Let's change the subject, shall we?" said Gus. "First things first, and then you can explain the whole thing to me."

With great formality he made all the introductions.

"This is Helen of Troy," he said, indicating the girl. She was wearing a navy blue sleeveless dress with white dots, made of a delicate fabric, with a dropped waistline, pleated behind. Falling below the knee, it was an elegant chemise, expensive, fine, and quite the latest thing in fashion. Her high-heeled shoes were white like her purse, which dangled from a long gilded chain. Her long nails were painted a bright, shiny pink. Her hair had been styled in a beauty salon with curlers, teasing, and spray.

"This is her brother, the famous Beelzebub Rincon Gallardo, alias Robert the Devil." A young man with unruly, tufty hair that no amount of pomade could control offered his hand to my grandmother. He was wearing an iridescent red-and-black bow tie. His short-sleeved shirt was white, his trousers checkered. One look at him told me what Grandma must be thinking: "This poor fellow has never made the acquaintance of a comb, and nobody's introduced him to the favorite aunt of every decent family, Madame Savoir Faire."

These two siblings with the ponderous surname looked like rich orphans left to fend for themselves. They had invested a small fortune in their clothing but still had the air of a couple of homeless dogs, of two flayed foxes from the middle of nowhere. He with his silly, skewed bow tie, and she with her starveling look and her need to impress the whole world, but with her dress half off one shoulder and her bra strap showing.

"Jack needs no introduction. He's already part of the family."

Uncle Gus then gave me my present, a beautiful Barbie with a stunning dress and a huge male doll, almost as big as me, dressed like a bridegroom.

"I brought my fiancée, and to make things even I brought you a fiancé so that you can't say I left you before you left me. What do you think of that?"

I thought the Barbie was wonderful, but I hated the male doll. And I hated Gus's sweetheart even more, though I said nothing. I stood there like a grinning idiot, while he took the girl's hand and held on to it, with her fingers encircling his. Now she looked less like a creature abandoned than an abandoned creature, the slut who had stolen my darling uncle.

A few minutes later I had accepted the idea that my doll boyfriend was quite charming, though he didn't hold a candle to Barbie. But Uncle Gus's girlfriend only got worse in my eyes, a tart to the core. I ran off to put my presents in my room, and immediately after they announced they were serving the appetizers.

The girl asked where the bathroom was, and my grandmother threw her a murderous glance. She considered it the height of bad breeding to use somebody else's bathroom, but she wasn't taking into account that they'd spent six hours on the highway. How could that slut, I kept asking myself, look so cool, so freshly showered, after battling dusty, bumpy roads in a speeding car? While she was in the bathroom, the doctor arrived, and a few minutes later the priest, without his soutane, dressed in a light-colored casual shirt, like any ordinary mortal.

They ate their appetizers on the terrace, watching the river glide by. The girl outdid herself in praising everything. Her

mouth was now bright red, as she'd put on lipstick in the bathroom. I was convinced she was lying, that she was only saying
this stuff to flatter Mama and Grandma. She wasn't particularly
smart, and didn't seem to realize that it was to her advantage to
win me over too. But she ignored me, as if I didn't matter. A
short while later she took out a small mirror to check her face,
as though some minor flaw might ruin the whole effect. I thought
she was horrible.

I stuck close to Gustavo, first standing by his side, then sitting on one arm of his chair. I finished up climbing onto his knees,
but, for the first time in our long acquaintance, he didn't pay me
much attention. At a quiet moment I said to him, "Let's go down
to the riverbank and I'll tell you all about old Luz."

He excused himself from the company and we went down
together. I told him what I'd seen, that Luz had awoken with
the stigmata of Christ, levitated, chair and all, and then disappeared by turning into pee in the darkness of her bathroom.

"The things you come out with! What you need is to get
out of this town as soon as you can. It's not possible that you
believe all this gobbledygook—"

"But I saw it with my own two eyes, Gus. I swear it. I'm
not lying or making things up. Honestly."

He took me by the hand. Now it was my hand he was
holding. Then he led me back to the others. China Jack had
everybody in stitches with a joke about the president, Lopez
Mateos. Uncle Gus said nothing for a moment or two and held
me on his knees, but after a moment he asked me to get up.
Then he got up himself and went for another martini and totally forgot about me. There were six people he had to attend
to, and one of them seemed to be worth double, maybe because of her disgustingly red mouth. I went by myself back down
to the side of the river to jump on the stepping stones before

they called us to eat, trying not to think about the slut and her expensive dress.

I'd hardly gotten settled at the table when a funny feeling came over my throat. I couldn't eat. The food just wouldn't go down. I made a terrific effort with the first bite and I coped with the prawn cocktail, overcoming the nausea I was feeling. But that was it. I couldn't manage another thing. I really did try, but it was no use. Gustavo congratulated me heartily on the G's on the bread, after Mama told him I was the one responsible, and then I asked to be excused from the table.

"What's wrong with the child?" asked Gustavo.

"Nothing. What could be wrong with her?" asked Grandma.

"She's feeling sick, Mama. Look at her. She's quite pale," said my mother.

"Yes, definitely not herself," Grandma agreed.

She shouldn't have said that because it was as if she'd given me permission to be sick in earnest. I ran to the bathroom and threw up. Then I tumbled into my hammock, sweating profusely. In a second or two I had become sick, truly sick. By the time they'd finished eating, I was burning with fever. It made me furious when Gustavo went out with China Jack and the tart to show them his failed projects. His favorite was a gigantic Ferris wheel. It had come to nothing because nobody in Agustini found it fun. "You go up so high in it you almost scrape your belly on the sky. You'd have to be crazy to want to go up that high." But then my thoughts wandered away from my indignation and how sick I was feeling, and for I don't know how long, I paid in my imagination a return visit to the basement, where men naked to the waist worked with flour.

"Got anything to lend me, dearie?" a voice was saying. I saw his hips pumping away inside the enormous mass of dough which responded to his movements as if it had a life of its own.

With rapt attention I checked out their faces and inspected all the oddities of the place. Those men didn't belong to this world. The huge masses with which they were playing didn't seem to belong here, either. Awkward, almost aquatic, kindred of the swamps, they slid and bounced like living creatures. The dough scared me more than the bakers did, though both filled me with indescribable horror.

19

Fever

Getting out of my sickbed four or five days later—and it really had been a bed, because the doctor had had them take down my hammock and for the first time in my life put me in an actual bed—everything had become blurry in my memory. The distortions produced by the fever had led me in turn to doubt the wild things that had happened before the fever, things that, far from questioning, I had hugged as mental treasures. I could no longer say for certain if the odd goings-on that had plagued our Sundays were factual. I had nobody to ask. All that remained in the kitchen of old Luz was her wooden chair. I felt desolate. I didn't know which of my memories I could trust. I asked my mother for Uncle Gustavo's whereabouts.

"Well, where do you suppose he is? He went to Mexico City."

"Is he going to get married soon?"

"Who is that old rascal ever going to marry?"

"That girl he brought with him."

"You don't understand a thing, do you?" she said. Her contempt was so profound she didn't even grace me with a glance.

At that moment I would have preferred her iciest glare to a straight nothing.

On the terrace overlooking the river, my nanny, Dulce, and my grandmother were shifting the cocoa plants left out to dry. The previous night it had rained, and as the ground wasn't completely flat, they had to prevent the cocoa plants from getting soggy in the pools that formed in the dips. Mama had shut herself up in her room, while Ofelia was cleaning mine without mercy, pouring out into it bucket after bucket of water and scrubbing it with a brush, intent on washing away the last bacteria from my illness, as if I'd been contaminated by the plague or some other highly contagious disease. She'd taken my sheets off to wash, and my mattress was lying outside in the sun.

I took refuge in the kitchen. As everything was topsy-turvy, I curled up at the feet of my missing Luz. There was no safer, cozier place. The living room was locked, as usual, and out on the patio the sun was beating down fiercely on the rocking chairs. Also, I felt that here, beside her chair, the spirit of old Luz would bring me comfort. I still wasn't strong, but not exactly tired, either. I hadn't brought my book with me, but I couldn't muster the energy to go to my room and get it and then return to this corner where there still lingered the shade of the woman who clapped her palms playfully together and who, until very recently, had celebrated my triumphs. Bored, I stretched out my hand toward her chair and stroked it. I touched it lightly a couple of times before realizing that, as I touched it, the chair detached itself from the floor and floated. Raising my head, I stood at one side of the chair. I put the palm of my hand on the seat and the chair rose a few inches off the ground. I took away my hand and the chair settled back gently onto the stone surface. I played a sort of yo-yo game with it, placing and removing my hand. I considered sitting in it and experiencing the levitation, but at the last moment I got scared. Old Luz had levitated in this chair just before she got the urge to pee that had meant her death.

I went out of the kitchen. I wanted to leave the house and check out the bandstand in the park and the roof of the market, to see if anything had really happened to them. I sauntered idly around the house, feeling sicker and sicker by the moment. That night the fever returned. Once again the doctor dislodged me from my hammock. I took a couple of weeks to recover fully from the typhoid. When at last I could leave the house again, feeling like the palest, skinniest girl in the world, the bandstand looked perfectly normal. I had a suspicion that its color, like that of the benches below it, wasn't quite the traditional white, but I couldn't swear to it. The ice-cream parlor still stood in its place, as did the furniture store and the roof of the market. It was as if nothing untoward had ever happened.

But the stalls of the Saturday market did display a novelty; they were now selling an abundance of desiccated birds and brilliantly colored feathers. That was enough to convince me that the events of the Sundays before my fever had been real.

By the time I got home, Luz's chair had disappeared. One of her granddaughters had laid claim to it, along with the crib and a pile of knickknacks that Grandma handed over without a qualm. I supposed they were going to sell off the lot as holy relics. Although their only connection had been to ask her for money and temporarily dump some unwanted child on her, they now were eager to make a fast penny out of her bits and pieces. I wondered who bought the underwear of Donã Luz. She had sewn them by hand herself. If her relatives had known the whole story of her demise, they doubtless would have marketed bottles of holy pee.

Some weeks later, we got a new cook, almost as old as Luz, though she was, in fact, her goddaughter. Her name was Lucita.

Mama and Dulce quickly baptized her Lucifer, and in a matter of weeks we were all calling her that. She combined the foulest of tempers with a superior talent in the kitchen. She produced *moles* and pumpkin-seed sauces and stews entirely new to our household. We became acquainted with a sloppy tomato stew, cactus leaves swimming in prawn juice with chile *pasilla,* and seafood in a hot pickle sauce, heavy with spices. She also cooked up more traditional dishes but gave everything a new twist. She drove Grandma crazy by smoking huge cigars that one of the market vendors used to bring her, along with her regular order for blue candles for the saint whose altar she had erected in her room, and a flagon of brandy.

She sneered at the loaves from the bakery. Instead, she baked heavy, compact bread once a week in the oven of our stove that previously we'd thought hardly capable of making even flan. According to Grandma, the gas she used in the process cost more than buying bread. According to Lucita, that wasn't her problem, and she carried on producing her tough, dense bread, as if deaf to Grandma's complaints. Sometimes she came up with a different bread, but it was even harder, made of dark flour and unground seeds, that her previous employer had taught her to make. She had been a German born in Tabasco, according to Lucita, but had sailed for Europe because she couldn't take any more of the heat in Cunduacan which was rotting her poor old creaking bones. It was my belief the woman had cooked up this excuse just to escape from the clutches of our marvelous but terrible Lucita.

She was a martinet with her assistants. And I say "assistants" because she demanded that Grandma hire someone beside poor Dulce, alleging that there were times she couldn't cope because the "little girl," meaning me, kept getting in the way. The great thing in her favor was that she filled our lives with the sweetness of honey, literally and metaphorically. She made unforgettable cakes, genuine marvels that belonged to traditions of latitudes far different from ours, as well as preparing jellies of very different flavors and textures. Her wine jelly was a work of genius, though her mamey jelly was second to none because she made it with nuts and fine brandy over a bed of eggs beaten into a batter that gradually absorbed it. It was perfect, just as her nut jelly was, as well as its cousin, the lemon mousse. She made the best Sacher torte that I've tasted in my whole life, and I've now been to Sacherhof itself to taste the original, so I know what I'm talking about. Her apple strudel was also beyond belief, but it all had to be eaten almost straight out of the oven, before the humidity with which we were constantly surrounded converted it into an unchewable, sticky goo.

Her cakes brought her such renown throughout the town that every afternoon we had visitors. On the slightest pretext, without a word of warning, my friends or those of Mama would drop by, the priest, the doctor, neighbors, the nuns, brought in by the delicious odors, to get their share of Lucita's baking. Not that she minded at all. She took it as part of her daily routine that folk would come by every afternoon to sample her cakes and other desserts. After a while she demanded yet another assistant from Grandma, and then another, and then another. The kitchen turned almost into a confectionery store. Dulce consoled herself for the loss of Doña Luz and her own displacement after Lucita's arrival by cramming herself with cookies and a thousand types of bread which she made with her own hands. Eating so much turned her into a creature of curves, not in the style of Mama but like the rotund women in the market. Soon she looked just like any other shapeless matron of the town. At sixteen she had the appearance of a mature woman. If Lucita were to die, we would have an immediate replacement in Dulce. Not that Lucita showed the slightest intention of dying. She wasn't related by blood to Doña Luz, but she gave the same impression of being likely to live for century after century. And appearances haven't proved deceptive. Today, thirty-odd years later, she is still there, the master cook, in the house in Agustini that I haven't gone back to in all these years.

1965

20

The Rains

I dashed out of school, desperate for a breath of fresh air. The ceiling fan in the classroom couldn't cut the thick atmosphere, merely making a useless noise and shifting portions of hot air from one side of the room to another, as if putting together a jigsaw it could never complete. The world was reduced to a single substantive: heat. Anything else to be said about it was buried before it could be voiced. All we could think was: "We're roasting." But if any words were fast enough to get out of our mouths, they immediately shriveled in the heat like moths in a candle flame. The nun had stopped talking. On the blackboard she had written three straightforward math problems. We had to write down the answers in our exercise books before we could go. She didn't have the strength to impose her will on us, but we didn't have the strength to defy her, either. All we wanted was to be out of there, but the idea of first doing three sums filled us with an almost insuperable lethargy. The hands of the clock seemed as motionless as the hot air, creaking around the face. The only sign of life in the room was the fan, and that was serving no purpose. One by one, we began drifting out of the classroom, almost giving off steam, only to find that the street awaited us with the glaring heat of a frying pan. Our sudden burst of vigor at getting out of the classroom was quashed by the fierce burning air.

Without thinking twice, I made for the river. I hadn't the energy to walk as far as my favorite bathing place, where a leafy tree and an enormous stone polished by the moving water made my entrances and exits easy, almost like at home. I and my class-mates once made a habit of going there together, on days like this, but for the past months they had been sticking to their clothes, as if a curse had been laid on them. They no longer came to swim in the river, and if I wanted to, I was obliged to splash around on my own, producing in them a contempt for this ac-tivity that they'd never shown in the past. Today their contempt didn't worry me. I felt dirty with the heat, battered by the heat, muddied with it. The heat made the insides of my thighs ache painfully. I had an overwhelming urge to soak myself in the coolness of the river. I picked out part of the bank where the stones were round and polished. I stripped down, quickly, effi-ciently, almost in a single movement, as if the mere sight of the water had reinvigorated my will. I ran barefoot across the long riverbed down to where the scanty water was still flowing, barely wetting the rocks, till with three short steps I reached the sec-tion where the water was still in full flow. There I plunged into the deep, welcoming cradle of water, into the deep pool formed by this backwater. The flow was abundant, even though we were in the dry season, and I submerged myself fully, face and hair, delighting in the merciful coolness of the water. I closed my eyes. It would be absurd to say I breathed deeply, but it was the first moment in that long day that my lungs really opened out. The burning air had been cramping them. Sunk in the river, my lungs escaped the torment of the oily, boiling air.

Reaching up my two hands, arms and fingers extended, I kicked my way back to the surface and floated faceup, with the eager water running off my body in rivulets. I decided to sit myself on the bottom of the riverbed and down I went, without giving myself time to put my hands underneath me to cushion my descent. A second later I felt an atrocious pain in my vulva, where the point of a rock had stabbed me. I felt the impact in my waist and belly. I saw risen in front of my eyes a single solid body running fearlessly to the river, without a drip of water on it, galloping rapidly, a single tense muscle there before my eyes, one suddenly blue and full of light that had abandoned me, robbing me of my natural strength, de-muscling me, if there is such a word, wounding me, stripping me naked.

There was no malice in the river. It was merely playing. It was skipping rope but sidestepping my body. My tense body was now detached from the riverbed, and the river glanced at it with an innocent smile and went its way. It fell gently over me, lifting me up and dropping me down, sending me to float among a thousand sizes of fishes scurrying across its breast. Now I watched them, both my eyes wide open. I pulled my head out of the water and breathed in the harsh, fiery noonday heat. My vulva hurt badly. What would happen if the river took me down a second time? I needed to get out. Driven by fear, I swam quickly for the bank. Scampering over the polished pebbles, I came to my clothes, with the water dripping off my skin, evaporating from contact with the sun. But I now had my own personal rivulet, a slender trickle of blood running down the inside of my thighs, marking on my body an earthy geography that I had not known I was endowed with. I watched the trickle; there it was, diluting itself in other, nearby waters. I cleaned it away with river water but it came back. The heat was so intense, the sun beating down with such force, that a few minutes' walking left me entirely dry. But my own private rivulet, although diminished, had not gone away, had not halted its movement, marking its borders with ever stronger force.

I clambered into my clothes but was careful not to get any stains on my dress. When I came to my panties, I discovered to my horror that they were marked by a dried-up dark brown streak. My only thought was not to walk through the streets dripping blood, so I put them on and hastened home, not at all bothered by the brutal sun that was slowing down the rest of the world.

There was nobody home when I got there. Dulce, Mama, Grandma were all out. Lucita was around but was slaving away with her army of assistants in the kitchen. Ofelia was scrubbing the terrace overlooking the river, and poor Petra was ironing the starched tablecloth in the hellishly hot laundry. I snatched up some clean panties, hid them under my clothes, and locked myself in the bathroom. The dark scab in the middle of my used panties had been softened up by a fresh trickle of blood. Where had that big stain come from? What had I been sitting on? I could recall nothing except for the seat of my school desk. I stopped thinking about it. But I kept on bleeding. I put a wad of white cotton inside the clean panties, to avoid dirtying them, and I went down to the river with the dirty panties hidden inside my clothes. I wrapped them around a small stone, screwing them into a tight ball, and threw them out as far as I could.

By mid-afternoon my private stream had not dried up. And it didn't dry up for three days. The first night, during which I was to leave stains on the white hammock and even a drop on the floor, I felt so tired I wasn't aware that Grandma was telling us an entirely different type of story. I didn't manage to hear its conclusion, and I'm not certain exactly how it went, because this one didn't have the usual tones and turns of phrase that she loved so much. That night the story was a succession of blurs I had trouble following and found it hard to impose any order on, but I still remember it, at least in part, with a clarity as if I'd heard it only yesterday, though I was ready to explode, unable to explain what was happening to me. That story went as follows.

"But let me stick to the point; that's enough of such airy-fairy talk. It was the time when my mother, her sisters, and my grandmother María del Mar were buying stuff for the bottom drawer of my aunt Pilar. She was a demon when it came to driving a bargain, always getting the best quality for the lowest price. Not that they told me so themselves, but I heard it from my nanny and my wet nurse. Back in those days no woman from a good family breast-fed her children. I can't imagine how your grandmother Pastora would have coped if they hadn't brought in these wet nurses, women who made a living out of breast feeding.

"Once again, I'm losing track, because this isn't the point of my story. I was trying to explain that when my mother, Pastora, her sisters, and my grandmother María del Mar were in Havana, this business with the stones and the water happened. Since they weren't around at the time, I never heard them mention it among themselves. So it couldn't have been them who told me how the stones and the water kept getting all mixed up, changing their appearances, without rhyme or reason, without respect for persons, producing a total muddle nobody could rely on. What was water one minute was a stone the next. During the night the fountains in the patios would start to make grating sounds, when the water suddenly turned into a clattering cascade of fine shiny pebbles, the sort you find snuggled into the bed of a river, or producing a real flood of pebbles when the basin of the fountain itself turned into water and all the pebbles came spilling out.

"Suddenly, if you went out riding, the way everybody did back then, to check on your farms or bring home some coal— you had to leave town in those days to get coal because the Indians weren't bringing it in, as they'd been forbidden to come into town after what had happened with Miss Antonia and Mr. Gutierrez (but that's a different story, which I'm not telling you now, because this one's about when the stones turned into water and the water into stones)—suddenly, as I was telling you,

you took a good look at Tostado Hill, that bald peak which looks so out of place around here where everything else is covered in green, since it was made out of solid rock from top to bottom, tough, enormous chunks of stone tossed up from the center of the earth, and a moment later, this hill, this pile of stones, was a waterfall hurtling down with no stopping it, then driven back up into place by the force of its own descent, and then starting to come back down again. It was such a remarkable sight that it became the fashion to make a daily trip out of town to see it, whether it was present as a solid mass of stone or as a tall, weird waterfall.

"The fishermen of the area were at their wit's end. They'd paddle out in their boats and drop their nets into the water, when suddenly, before they could decide whether it was water going or rocks coming, they'd find themselves stranded in a frightful rocky landscape, unable to move forward or backward, and not interested in jumping out of their boats to chase their prey because of the heat wave. The kids had fun catching the fishes jumping around the stones that the river and the three lakes had turned into. And the hunters of crocodiles and alligators had a rare old time of it and really cashed in. All this I'm describing to you came to an end as soon as my mother, Pastora, and my grandmother María del Mar returned from Cuba. It turned into no more than a memory, just one among many, but what I really wanted to talk about was what happened next, because, as you're all aware . . .''

22

First Night

The next morning Dulce cleaned up the drop of blood and washed my nightdress and my hammock, so that no sign of my period remained. She didn't say a word about it but left in my chest of drawers a bag of cotton for me to find, and by the side of the chest put a woven wastebasket, freshly purchased, and by the side of that, on the edge of the mirror frame, small brown paper bags.

The second night, when I still felt like dying from my strange fall in the river, because of the shooting pains I was experiencing in my gut, Grandma told us a weird story that I listened to without a moment's inattention, giving it all my energy so as not to fall victim to the stomach pains, until, that is, I promptly sank into a profound sleep, without understanding where Grandma's story was headed, or what its true subject matter might be or why she had chosen that particular night to describe a place whose existence she had never before breathed a word of, a place totally alien to those we were used to taking our nightly strolls through, places like Agustini, but more nightmarish, wilder, far less tamable.

23

Grandmother's Story

"You're all aware that far from the Costa de Progreso, on the way to Carmen Beach, there once existed the Archipelago del Berro, that is, until the Great Wave, the one that preceded the cholera epidemic of 1846, swept it away in a matter of seconds.

"My father had heard talk of it from his nanny, who was part black, part Chole, part Zapotec, and part white. She was dark-skinned all over her body, but her fingertips were light-colored, and her nipples were those of a blonde. She had the swaying gait typical of the coast, but her slender thighs came from Oaxaca, her great big boobs from the north, and her frizzy hair from the blacks. Behind my grandparents' back, she had described to my father the activities of the Evil One, how the dead in New Orleans came back to life, and how dogs gobbled up naughty children. Her descriptions were packed with convincing details but, all the same, so fantastically preposterous that no adult with a grain of common sense would credit them for a moment. The story about the Archipelago del Berro was included in her tales, but there was a significant difference. The Evil One, the child-swallowing dog, the resurrected dead, all belonged to a world that doesn't exist, but the archipelago was the pure truth, a place you could touch.

"The Archipelago del Berro, his nanny told him, was situated not far from the coast. Any afternoon he wanted they could hire him a kid to take him there. It was just a matter of his parents dropping him off at the harbor and once they let him out of sight and mind, they could make the trip in three hours.

"Not content with merely mentioning the place and describing it, his nanny more than once got involved in arranging to go see the place.

"'The First Communion of your aunt Dorita's daughter is coming up. They'll be bound to take us to Paraíso. After breakfast the grown-ups will be busy preparing lunch, and you and me can slip away so that you can set eyes on it, and see for yourself that I'm telling the truth . . .'"

24

Second Night

However hard I try, I still can't recall the tone in which Grandma described the Archipelago del Berro to us. It's not just that I can't remember what it was like or even the point of the story she started to tell us before I nodded off, but I can't remember at all how she threaded the words together, how she used words to describe something that lay outside the realm of words. I'll do it in my own way. To the observing eye the Archipelago del Berro was exactly like every one of the graceless islands that dot the coastline of the southern section of the Gulf of Mexico, an area of sea spotted with bits of flat land, of hardly any width, surrounded by shallow waters. The islands are marshy. So marshy it's hard to say where dry land ends and the water begins. It would be an impossible task to map these islands because they aren't stationary. In the rainy season they're flooded, and only in the dry season do they emerge from the surrounding waters, and even then not fully.

The Archipelago del Berro had no vegetation whatever. Not even a single one of those shrubs that can sprout as soon as they get a direct dose of sunlight and then survive underwater for weeks or even months. The sandy soil was shiny but dark-colored, as if composed of thousands of shattered crystals. But its real uniqueness didn't lie in either the barrenness or the brilliant shine. You had to set foot on the archipelago to realize what was special about this place, to know where its power, its charm, lay. When you walked over the surface, whether your feet were wet or dry, the ground opened up, sucking at your feet, trapping them. It let them go only after it had kissed your foot, your ankle, your shin, your knee. Nothing above the knee. But at the same time there was a scorching wind blowing, taking you prisoner physically. It invaded the rest of your body. One half of your leg might have escaped the heavy earth, but the stifling grasp of the breeze wouldn't let go of you. Just walking there felt like swimming, entering into another body, being submerged in fresh dough.

According to my grandfather's nanny, anybody who had experienced the archipelago was marked for life. Some people got so hooked on the place that they refused to get back in the boat and go home. "This place delights in you and lets you delight in it—I never want to leave!" they'd cry. The inevitable outcome was that they died there of hunger and thirst, but without feeling the least pang of hunger or thirst, with no feeling of parched lips or aching guts, simply reduced to a surface of sensual skin, receiving hugs, delighting in caresses, fully embraced but suffering no ill effects, a total enjoyment.

That's why his nanny so often told my grandfather that in front of the harbor of Paraíso stood the genuine Paradise, for that archipelago was the living antithesis of the filthy port.

As soon as my grandfather reached manhood, though he still had the look of a child, he didn't wait for one of his nanny's pretexts to visit the archipelago. Those pretexts were often talked about but never materialized, anyway. When his voice started to break, one minute squeaky, the other booming deep, and his chin started to grow a scruffy fuzz you couldn't yet dignify with the name of a beard . . .

It was at this age, Grandma said, when her father looked a lot younger than he really was . . . But at this point I fell asleep, without learning if her father set foot on the soil that was out to kiss him or if he even saw the archipelago and found out for himself where it got its name or what he had done that deserved to be commemorated in one of Grandma's stories, which had seemed to be about something else, anyway.

25

Third Night

The third night of the bleeding I believed the river had produced in me, I heard my grandmother's story right through to its conclusion. Afterward I fell asleep but without getting rid of the ache in my belly. It finally left me wide-awake and I had to get out of my hammock and go to the bathroom, something I'd never done before. Ever since childhood I'd managed to sleep through the night without peeing, never leaving my hammock for any reason whatever. With my period pains, though I didn't know to call them that, I made my dark way to the bathroom. On the central patio my grandmother was lying asleep on her shawl, floating, suspended a yard off the ground. Beneath her, stretched out on her rebozo, without any concern for scorpions, ants, or worms, my nanny, Dulce, lay sprawled on the ground like a small dog. Her rebozo did not share the ability of Grandma's shawl to float freely in the air.

I went to the bathroom and then out of curiosity peered into my mother's room. She was asleep in her hammock, lying peacefully, her arms open. In the darkness which the moonlight barely disturbed I thought I counted three naked legs.

I went back to my hammock and lay down restlessly, unable to fall asleep. I got the idea of retelling the story that Grandma had told that night, and in the process of retelling it I did manage to fall asleep at some point.

26

Growing Up

In a flash my growing body was filled with oddities. Beside the little toe on my right foot there sprouted a roundish growth. It seemed to be made of a hornlike substance. First it was round and smooth, but within a few days it had acquired a point, a horn.

That weekend Uncle Gustavo came to visit us. This time he brought no companions, not even his shadow, China Jack. Nor did he bring any of his crazy ideas for the kind of projects he'd undertaken in Agustini as a youngster, things like the disastrous Ferris wheel, the factory for assembling handbags of crocodile skin, the chocolate and eggnog factory, his henhouses, and the production of a miracle cure for baldness. Luckily, on each of these ventures, for all his losses he'd managed to recoup his investment, or so at least he claimed. The sole exception was the Ferris wheel, which he described as "his favorite child, his most brilliant but his most selfish one, because it didn't bring in a red cent, the rascal, it was a total write-off."

Gustavo spent virtually all his time out at the farm with Grandma, checking out God knows what, but I did have him to myself for a few minutes. I asked if he knew anything about creatures with horns on their feet.

"There aren't any gods with horns on their feet. There are some with wings on their feet and they use them to go flying around, but as far as I remember, none with horns. It'd be unnec-

essary to invent one with horns. What would be the point? It would
be a useless sort of monster, ridiculous. Don't you think so?"

I didn't dare say that I had a horn growing out of the side
of my right foot. When all was said and done, it wasn't a very
big horn. Its length was about a sixth of an inch, but I had spent
so much time staring at it that I had begun to imagine myself a
being with an abundant horn on my right foot, though careful
examination revealed only a small formation about a tenth of an
inch wide.

My smooth, fair hair had now turned dark and curly. I was
cursed with a strange, wild mane that my nanny, Dulce, could
not keep under proper control and that I myself could not organize into any semblance of elegance. It was as if my hair had been
switched with somebody else's. I spent so much time observing
my damned horned foot and curly hair that other changes in
appearance escaped my notice. For example, it took me a long
time to realize that I had developed a woman's breasts. What
alerted me to the fact was that one day I couldn't fasten the blouse
of my school uniform.

It was an old blouse. My other three were roomier and I
preferred them. But Petra had taken sick and my clean clothes were
not getting back to my wardrobe, so I had to grab the tight blouse
I hadn't used for some time. I couldn't fasten the buttons. Tugging and tugging at the fabric, I became aware of my two protu-
berances. I felt so embarrassed by their presence that I didn't want
to go to school and to give myself an excuse not to, I got diarrhea.
I managed to avoid thinking about them for the rest of the day,
spending the time to-ing and fro-ing between my bedroom and
the bathroom, with a dribble of excrement that kept my mind off
other things, but whose source was nothing but my furious astonishment. I had given myself this angry diarrhea.

I really was furious. I wanted to know nothing of this sub-
cutaneous invasion. Against my will I was forced to recognize

the growth of pubic hair, of hair under my arms, and of the narrowing of my waist. I felt I was living proof of the invasive thievery that precedes physical assault.

I had never been one to have lots of friends. A few gluttons from my class showed up at the house in the afternoons to gobble some of Lucifer's cakes, but that was the limit of their interest. They called themselves my friends to facilitate their appetites. They'd play around with my Barbies and I'd give them some fleeting attention, but soon I'd lose interest. I'd throw myself onto my bed or settle down on the bench at its foot, lost in what I was reading, ignoring them. As soon as they'd finished dessert and got bored with the stiff-limbed dolls, they were on their way. They'd come for the sake of the food and the dolls, not for me. Because of what was happening to my developing body, I shut myself in my bedroom with increasing frequency and I had not even the company of those fitful visitors. They felt less and less welcome in the house, not so much for my hostility, I suspect, but because they were outgrowing the dolls and the other toys. Not even the continued excellence of Lucifer's cakes was enough to keep them coming. The afternoons I spent partly in reading, partly in examining my physical misfortunes, and for the first time in my life I caught myself sighing over somebody. I had somehow gotten it into my head that in some corner of the world dozens of potential friends were waiting for me to come and chat with them about the hundreds of ideas that were starting to force themselves on me. I sighed for those somebodies, at the very moment I was insisting on the gap between me and my actual friends. I'd decided that I'd absolutely nothing to say to them. They spent the afternoons playing around with makeup, trying on wigs and clothes, and gossiping about the three boys from the town they wanted to go on dates with.

I wasn't the only girl who dreamed of getting out of Agustini, but I was the only one who dreamed of getting out for my own

particular reason. The others wanted out to go chasing boyfriends
and husbands, the two boundaries of their world. We were only
twelve years old, but our whole outlook on life was reduced to
marriage. Ahead of us lay three lifeless years. The town's school
did not go beyond the primary division. For a secondary education we had to go to Puebla or Villahermosa or Mérida. Nobody took seriously the idea of doing our secondary studies in
the town's official secondary school, since it involved being surrounded by scruffy Indians and sharing the single classroom where
the one teacher had to teach all three grades.

Mama and Grandma had considered sending me to Puebla,
to the boarding school where six of my schoolmates would be
going. The idea did not appeal to me in the slightest. Mama and
I had been to see the school. We made a lengthy journey, hop-
ping on and off ferries, and had an interview with the nuns in
Puebla where they'd given me an entrance exam that consisted
of responding orally to catechism questions. My spelling was of
no account. The school taught cooking, embroidery, knitting,
housekeeping, and French. I could have learned all that at home,
apart from the French, though Mama had in fact studied French
with those nuns and spoke it fluently. She owed her fluency to
having spent time in Europe, where she got pregnant with me,
but that was a subject never mentioned at home, as if silence
could undo it and leave me as nobody's child. On Fridays the
nuns organized tea dances, attended by boys from the Marist
high school, the cream of Puebla society. The subjects taught
to the boarders were cooking, etiquette, makeup, and hairdress-
ing, and they killed two birds with one stone by screening out
from the tea dances all but the most eligible young men. There
wasn't the slightest doubt that by the time the girls were ready
to graduate from secondary school, they would have reached
an understanding with some good catch approved by the strict
gaze of the nuns.

27

The Holiday Rains

The dry season had lasted longer than normal and our towns-people were starting to get nervous. The heat had become intolerable; dust kept us shut inside our homes; the river had dwindled to practically nothing; and the sound of rain was merely a delightful memory. In our part of the world it usually rained every year, abundantly, noisily, exaggeratedly. Our climate was always one of benevolent opulence. We were people of the rain, hardened to floods and water in excess. Our ancestors had lost their scales in the course of evolution, but they still had the souls of fishes. We awaited impatiently the arrival of the rainy season, wanting to feel raindrops on our skin at every hour of the day, eager to cool off, if it isn't too much of a paradox to say so, in the pools of air that had turned into pure dampness, if not precisely into water.

It should have been raining by now, but it wasn't. Our skins were stinging with the dryness. Our throats were on fire, as if we'd spent weeks breathing sand through our gills. St. John's Day was almost on us and we still hadn't seen a drop of water. The traveling fair had installed itself in town, untroubled, for the first time ever, by the rains. The usual trucks had arrived, loaded with bumper cars, the whip disassembled into its various sections, the sideshows with their bizarre fake animals, the goat with five legs, the cow with two heads, the green sheep, the dartboards and the games of marbles, along with their gaudy prizes, the trucks of the magician and the turtle-woman, and one truck with a large tower in its middle that now reminds me of a lifesaving tower but back then looked like a hellish machine for shaking up the hearts of all the kids in town, spinning them around more vigorously than the whip and whirling them higher than even my uncle's despised Ferris wheel.

The fair was set up for the evening of St. John's Day and tickets went on sale. I headed first of all to the tower to find out what it was and how it worked, to learn what perverse pleasures it had in store for us.

A loudspeaker announced that since so many of us were waiting to go up the tower—practically the whole population of the town, apart from the nuns, the priest, and the servant girls— we'd have to exercise patience before we could have our fun, since it accepted riders in groups of ten and took its time doing so. In front of me were a lot more than ten customers, so I bought a ticket for the nearest sideshow: the turtle-woman. She had a human head and the body of a water turtle. From the bottom of a fish tank, but with her hair suspiciously dry, she told us that she had been transformed into this monster for disobeying her parents. She was blowing bubbles in the water, while doing her best to look regretful for her misdemeanors, when suddenly the sky burst open and down came the deluge. Her head got a good soaking. Luckily the fish tank in which she was doing her stuff wasn't filled with water. We all burst out laughing, but the turtle-woman maintained throughout her solemn, tragic look typical of a Papantec Indian, priestlike and scornful. She kept up her air of repentance, though we could all see now that the trick was done with mirrors.

The downpour lasted only a minute.

The tower had been responsible for it; it was a rainmaking machine. Fishes though we folk of Agustini were, we agreed that the following morning we would buy tickets in groups of ten and that we'd keep the night dry so that we could enjoy the fair. The turtle-woman, submerged in her enormous fish tank, did not get a second drenching. Only those of us who had gotten in first had seen through the illusion; the clever placement of mirrors let her stay dry, although to all appearances she was condemned to an underwater existence for "having disobeyed her parents."

The next morning the rain poured down in sporadic bursts. It was unusual in that it was not accompanied by thunder and lightning, or even by a wind. Huge drops of rain as big as golf balls fell on the town and its immediate surroundings. The rest of the storm's paraphernalia did not show up; there wasn't a crack of thunder or a gust of wind or even clouds blotting out the sun, while these monster drops fell out of a clear sky. The rain was so dense that we could barely make out the entrancing groups of gigantic rainbows that glittered in the sky.

The rain did not reach our farm, so Grandma entered the tower to ask if they could extend its rainmaking powers to irrigate it, or would it be necessary to move the tower to the farm? But this last suggestion was totally impractical, as the dreadful state of the roads precluded all possibility of moving it there.

"Buy fifty sets of ten tickets, and you'll see rain like you've never seen it before," said the manager of the fair.

Grandma didn't hesitate for a second. She paid him the equivalent of fifty sets of ten tickets and asked him to hold off the rain to give her time to get home without getting soaked. She had barely gotten through the door when the skies burst open. It was a rain like no other that fell on Agustini, and that was a town used to extraordinary rains.

We were approaching the final days of the school year, and nothing was allowed to interfere with our attendance or interrupt the lessons and exams. The test papers for the final exams of the primary division had arrived from the Secretary of Education and the nuns wanted us to pass them with flying colors, to avoid any chance that official inspection would oblige them to show up at school without their religious garments and adopt a pose of amnesia, for fear of any questions about their actually being nuns. The tremendous rains had started to abate. We had been unable to speak as they fell because of the sheer noise of the downpour, but a terrified nun ordered us all home, crying, as they usually did when Nature unleashed its forces, "It's the end of the world, the end of the world. Pray, girls, pray!"

Her reaction was total folly. If there had been anything untoward in that dense downpour or if any danger had been heading our way, we were safer at her side than scattered around the town, but no sooner were her panicky words out of her mouth than we all did have to run for it, while she darted off to find refuge with her fellow nuns behind the high walls of the convent, racing past the church, as they had all agreed to do in case of extreme need, or danger, or threats leveled against the Christian faith, or against their own humble persons'.

The river had burst its banks. I walked home, dodging its roaring violence. Going past the bakery, somebody tall and paunchy grabbed me by the waist and lifted me off the ground, without giving me a chance to let out even a howl of alarm or scream for help or run for my life.

A fat hand over my mouth stopped me from calling out. I'd no idea what was happening. I recall only the basement of the bakery, a ridiculous tugging, the hands of the man searching through my clothes, my screams once his hands got busy with something other than my mouth, my feet slipping in the wet flour, the crash of his body against me when he fell against a table with the flour on it. And then the secondary school teacher came in and let out a shout when he saw what was going on.

"Cut that out!"

The man let me go.

"Can't you see she's just a kid? What's gotten into you? I know you've probably only got flour for brains, but what about your heart? Tell Delmira you're sorry."

"I thought it was her mother," the man answered, stuttering, by now at quite a distance from me.

"Are you blind as well as stupid? And what's with you other guys?" It was then I saw the rest of the bakers who surrounded us, dressed in white, naked to the waist, their eyes wide, as they stood in the middle of the cloud of light. I also realized that my school blouse was open and I fastened it, pulling down the vest that the man had forced upward. To my dismay I had peed myself with fright and my panties were soaked. "This is outrageous, you guys. Outrageous! Come here, girl."

He took me by the hand and, without letting it go, accompanied me up the stairs that I had no recollection of coming down. Outside, the town was still suffering the after-effects of the turbulent downpour. People were pouring out bucketfuls of water from their patios and placing sacks of salt at the doors of their houses. They cursed me as I went by, without my realizing that they blamed Grandma for this torrential storm. I felt they were insulting me for what had just happened at the bakery, as if my conduct required their rebukes. My legs were all a-dither and my breathing disjointed. The teacher still hung on to my hand. This friend of the Indians had taken responsibility for me, rescuing me from something terrible, something I could not even imagine. For one moment I felt extreme shame before him. He had seen me with all my clothes disordered, while that disgusting hand was humiliating me with its gropings. Indifferent to my distress, almost carrying me along and not allowing me the breather that my condition might seem to require, he hurried me along like a graceful skein of silk, through the streets of

Agustini, straight to the bandstand in the park, where he invited
me to have an ice cream. He sat down in front of me to eat his
ice. He had ordered me a double lemon.

"If you want to cry," he said, sitting there, "you can, Delmira.
You have my permission. If anybody asks what happened to you,
I'll cover for you. Invent what you like, that you stumbled and
fell, that the river nearly carried you away. Anything you like."

I didn't speak. The ice cream was working wonders, as was
the attentive glance of the teacher. Ice cream and attention were
putting me back together. Of the innumerable ice creams I had
gobbled down in the course of my life, none had had this effect.
And never before had I seen a look like that of the teacher, so
warm, so trustworthy that it inspired in me a peaceful confidence.

"Don't speak if you don't want. But if you feel like it, bawl
your head off."

"I've nothing to cry about," I said in a self-collected tone.

"Wow, what are you made of, kid? Don't you feel anything?"

"Of course I feel things. But I'm not stupid. I stop feeling
them, if they feel nasty. Anyway, I like to be tough. Only tough
girls like me can outlast bony women."

The teacher laughed. "You've got flour on your back. Let
me dust it off."

"I've also got dripping-wet socks," I thought and after a
second added out loud, "I'd better go home and change, but . . ."

"You want to go?"

I shook my head. He got up and with a few gentle pats
knocked the flour out of my hair and my clothing. He looked
down at my feet.

"Your socks will soon dry out. I know, we'll get another
ice cream, we'll sit on a bench in the park, you can take off your
shoes and socks, and you can tell me the story of your life. How
about it?"

He didn't wait for my reply. He ordered two more ices, paid for them, and made me a sign to follow him. We sat under a solid shelter and looked at the church.

"So?"

"So what?"

"You're just finishing your primary education. What plans do you have now?"

"My grandmother wants to send me to Puebla to learn things she could have taught me here herself. It makes me want to puke, just to think about taking classes in cooking and embroidery and knitting. What's the point?"

"You have friends at school?"

"You've got to be kidding! The girls in my class have their heads full of sawdust. There's not one of them even remotely like a human being, not a single one. Can you believe it? All they talk about is getting married, about boyfriends, what their house is going to be like, how many kids they're going to have, if they want their first kid to be a boy or a girl, where they're going to go for their honeymoon."

"Why don't you come to the secondary school with me? Do you like math?"

"I can do math faster than the nuns can."

"Well, that's not saying a lot. Do you like to read?"

"It's what I like best. I read while the nuns are making a mess of explaining how to do sums."

"What books do you read?"

"Those in the study at home. My uncle Gustavo's old books. *The Treasure of Youth. The Adventures of William. The Three Musketeers.* Rocambole and Jules Verne. *Les Miserables . . .*"

"Which do you prefer, *Around the World in Eighty Days* or *Doctor Jekyll and Mister Hyde*?"

"*Doctor Jekyll.*"

"Sherlock Holmes or Robin Hood?"

"I'm not sure. Robin Hood, I guess."

"Anybody else in your class like to read?"

"Not as far as I know."

"You're going to come to the secondary school and study with me."

"You've got to be crazy. My grandmother wouldn't dream of allowing it."

"Father Lima owes me a few favors. He'll make sure you come to my school. Your grandmother isn't going to say no to him. And not to Gustavo either, because he's sure to approve. Afterward you can go study for your university entrance in the city. Then you'll go to the university, finish your degree there, and you'll be ready to take on the world. How does that sound?"

"I don't know . . . well, yes . . . I like it a lot."

The sound of his voice pleased me better and better. I liked him more each moment that passed. He was a seductive fellow, ugly and skinny but with a definite appeal, a snake charmer, a pied piper. He was much wittier than China Jack and far more intelligent.

"I've a dream that my uncle Gustavo would take me away with him to the city as soon as I finish my primary schooling, and I'd get my high school education there . . ."

"What do you want to study?"

"I want to be an archaeologist."

"Heaven help us! You've told your grandmother that?"

"I don't talk to her. I've never talked to her. All day long she's cleaning and cleaning or doing the accounts of the farm. What does she need all those accounts for?"

"That farm of hers is worth a fortune."

"I'd like to go away with Gus. He's nothing like the rest of them."

"Gus couldn't take you away right now. But in three years' time it'll be a different story. He'll be delighted to do it. Ready to go home now?"

"No way!"

"Do you like music?"

"What? The stuff on the radio?"

He laughed. He asked me no more questions. All he said was "Let's go to my place." I put my shoes and socks back on. They were practically dry. We left the park bench and walked off, chattering nonstop, toward his house. The sun was shining as if it had never rained in Agustini.

28

The Teacher's House

The teacher's house was very different from mine and from other houses in town. It didn't look like those I'd seen on my trips with the priest, either, the cool, dark houses of the Indians, rounded off without corners, made of adobe, and with a roof of palm branches, or the enormous homes of overseers and ranch owners, with lofty ceilings, surrounded by verandas, with inside patios and an endless succession of rooms. It had nothing in common with the houses of my cousins in Puebla or Villahermosa, city houses of two or more stories, with balconies, comfy chairs, rugs or carpets on the floors, noisy air-conditioning, staircases with handrails, interior hallways, roofed-over patios, furniture that was either antique or grotesquely trendy, and a host of bathrooms that made sense only if the idea was to trap vampires in the vast number of mirrors.

The door of the teacher's house opened directly onto a living room with a mosaic floor and two windows, not a balcony, over-looking the street. It was a shadowy room, cool and furnished with armchairs with pointed feet. An unusual silence reigned there because there wasn't a constant coming and going of people as in other houses, including my own. There it wasn't uncommon to see the seller of honey sniffing around the door of my bedroom,

or the boy who sold lottery tickets, or the lady who brought the
bedsheets and the gigantic kitchen linens, all embroidered with the
U of my family's surname. People came and went. They dropped
in unannounced and sometimes overstayed their welcome. The
only ones who could be guaranteed to leave the house at the first
opportunity were the Indians who had come from the farm with
their fat overseer, but even these stayed to drink a soda pop offered
by old Luz with her smiling face or the wretched Lucifer cursing
them under her breath. The Indians crouched on the floor of the
kitchen and the overseer sat facing the grinder on the table, without removing his hat. When I was very small, the overseer used to
arrive on horseback, mounted on a handsome sorrel he called "the
apple of his eye." Later, it was one of the trucks for transporting
coffee that dropped him off at our door, with the wood of the
siderails constantly creaking away, since he never bothered to switch
off the engine. The trucks had their individual names, of course,
written below the tailgate in thick black letters: MY FINAL TRIP or
BUTTERFLY OF THE HIGHWAY.

Of all the houses that I'd entered before the teacher's, the
quietest had been Elbia's. Her grandfather owned a downtown
furniture store which supplied the whole area with mattresses,
wardrobes, tables of shiny Formica, headboards, bureaus, and
such, and his son had opened up branches of the same tasteless
business in Villahermosa, Tampico, and finally in Mexico City.
But the grandfather had suffered a paralysis, both physical and
mental, in some muddy affair in an out-of-the-way corner of
Africa. His son, Elbia's uncle, the rich furniture dealer, and the
grandfather, the provincial furniture dealer, had gone on a hunting
trip with the idea of both shooting lots of animals and returning
with items of interior decor. They were planning to bring back
stuff to liven up the look of their stores: stuffed heads of lions,
elephant feet to use as umbrella stands, tusks, and the skins from
zebras and tigers. And they did return with a pile of stuff, but the

grandfather had suffered some unspeakable accident, something to do with a kidnapping attempt, if I'm not mistaken, and now he was reduced to a ghastly piece of furniture himself. But even there, in that house of sickness and quietly longed-for death, people came and went, though without too much hustle and bustle. At my home the birdseller used to come in whistling, after he'd propped up his cages against the housefront, the man selling cheeses came in with a song on his lips, the woman selling threads and embroidery came in reciting her prayers, often mistaking our house for the convent, and not without good cause, as their styles were similar. In Agustini silence was an extinct species. All the houses buzzed like beehives. People fluttered in and out, conducting nonstop conversations, doing their accounts, offering to sell live crabs, prawns, and crayfish from the river and green papayas marinated in black sauce, or wanting to buy our eggnog, to cadge a piece of cake or a mouthful of something, to give somebody a hand beating cream into butter.

What a contrast to the little house where the teacher lived with his aunt! The metal door of his house was kept shut, as it gave directly onto the living room, as in Indians' houses. It wasn't as dark as the windowless houses of the Mayans who lived in other parts of Tabasco, but it admitted much less light than ours. Entering that house was like entering another town, entering a mestizo settlement of a type not known in Agustini. All the objects inside it rested on one another. The ashtray leaned on the windowsill; returning the coffee cup to the table produced a sharp and scary *puck!* sound. Things in that house had a secondary body. Their nature possessed something strange. There were no flower vases, no plastic flowers as in the majority of houses, no natural flowers as in our house and the priest's. There were no statues on the furniture, no clown like the one that first appeared in the living room of Doña Gertrudis de las Vegas, Grandma's friend whom we used to visit now and then. "It's a compassionate visit,"

Grandma used to explain. "The poor dear's lost everything she had, it's a crying shame, just look at how she lives!" There were no bells there like those in my house, no Lladro figurines like in our house, no statues of the Virgin that the nuns had assiduously collected and foisted on the priest.

Instead, he had an uncountable number of books, scattered here and there throughout the whole house, on bookshelves, on tabletops, on various parts of the floor, but without the accumulations of fluff and dust that gathered like a perverse fungus around neglected books in our house, where I was the only one to bother with them. There were also things that never got inside our house: newspapers and magazines. When Gustavo lived in Agustini, he would go to the café and read the papers and magazines he bought in the arcades, but he invariably left them there for the waiters to read or toss into the garbage.

Among the pile of propped-up things, the teacher also possessed something else forbidden to the rest of us. I can still recall vividly the time Gustavo tried and failed to get the thing working in our house. It was a record player. He'd bought it in Campeche, where he did a fair amount of business, and brought it home, along with a good number of cumbersome 78s, one of which had been damaged on the bumpy journey home. The machine was a handsome, modern portable Panasonic, in a light green case, with two speakers in its lid and the turntable in its base. Gustavo assembled it carefully and positioned the speakers which were connected by dark brown wires to the machine, but for all his efforts, no matter what he connected or disconnected, he couldn't get a sound out of it. He checked this and that, and was considering taking it back to the dealer who'd brought it in from the States, when he realized that the needle wasn't making contact with the surface of the record. Hence the absence of sound. He tried to lower the arm by weighting it down with a one-cent coin on its flat top. No go. He used every coin of our national currency. Still the needle floated in midair. He then tried an American quarter, but all he succeeded in doing was producing a few bars of a song and then ruining the record. The teacher had this very same type of record player, but his worked, and on it we listened to songs that are still engraved in my memory. They were by Bob Dylan. The needle worked perfectly and, even though the records themselves were lighter, bigger, and thinner than those brought by Gustavo, the sound was flawless.

The other resident of the house, his aunt, seemed much older than my grandmother. She was a spinster who had looked after her nephew since he was a baby. Now she worked as a teacher at the public school, and was known in the town as Miss Ramírez Cuenca. The family was restricted to the pair of them, another oddity in our part of the world, where our relations branched out far and wide, ad nauseam. One afternoon, I recall, my grandmother decided to recite to me the genealogical tree of the Ulloas. It extended from the founding of Agustini to the present day, constantly widening, until it seemed there wasn't a single family of good standing that wasn't connected to us. The town was inhabited by a vast legion of our cousins, uncles, aunts, nephews, and nieces.

I'm not sure how much time we spent together at his house, jumping from one record to the next, from Debussy, who didn't really turn me on, though the teacher was crazy about him, to what did turn me on: Joan Baez, Simon and Garfunkel, Scott McKenzie's "San Francisco," and Oscar Chavez. But our time together was enough to restart my calendar. Everything I was used to, my home, the school, the town of Agustini, was consigned to the past. We didn't even have a radio at home. What I heard on the radios in the market was nothing but out-of-date Mexican music and pseudo-tropical groups. When they did feel like listening to something modern, they switched stations to pick up mawkish balladeers or the counselor who dispensed sentimental advice to the single women of Agustini on a program called "Healing Your Heart." My grandmother declared that since time began there hadn't been a bigger fraud than that chatterbox. She couldn't understand why the girls took her so seriously. As for me, I couldn't stand to listen to her. There was something sickly in her voice that drove me wild. But my mother and Dulce just adored her. They'd find an excuse to slip out of the house at the time of the broadcast and stick their ears to a radio. They'd stand in front of the radio in the furniture store or at the market and listen to it with reverence. The second she stopped talking and was replaced by songs, the pair of them would dash home, racing back before Grandma suspected the real reason for their absence. Then, when Lucifer had come to work in our kitchen, she brought a radio with her. She kept it in her room, and while the program was on, there was no finding Dulce. She was in Lucifer's room, her ear stuck to the radio. The poor dear cherished some fantasy of finding a man, and maybe even of marrying one, though, to my knowledge, she never found any man particularly to her liking.

While we listened to the records, we were munching on a ham sandwich or two. It was made with factory-produced white bread with a soft crust, something I'd never eaten in my entire life. Sometimes a classmate would bring sandwiches to school to eat at break time, but sandwiches were not part of my family's diet. The usual thing to eat at break was a tortilla fried by the nuns. They sold them at the door of the school both to the students and to the not inconsiderable number of passersby who had gone out of their way just to get their teeth into this delicious food.

It was now time for me to go home. The teacher's aunt had been out and she came back with the news that the Ulloa family had been apprised of the incident at the bakery. Then she went out again to put a stop to the gossip that was spreading like wildfire throughout the town. Though she was ex-

tremely upset by this, I wasn't in the least bothered, and I refused to give it a second thought. On my way home the teacher
was talking to me, but I scarcely heard a word of it, because
inside my head "Blowing in the Wind" was playing at a vol-
ume that overwhelmed anything coming in from outside. I also
failed to notice that the teacher wasn't with me when I stepped
inside the house.

I ran into my bony relatives in the patio. They were both
talking heatedly, so heatedly that at first they didn't notice my
entrance. "Hi, you two!" I called out cheerily. On hearing my
voice Mama slipped out of her hammock and, forgetting her usual
feline gait, raced off to her bedroom, smothering a tearful groan
that the pattering of her heels could not fully mask. My grandmother, however, remained rooted to the spot, staring at me.
"What on earth is wrong with them?" I thought. On hearing
my voice, Dulce emerged from the kitchen, with her mouth still
stuffed with some goody or other, and came hurtling toward the
patio. When she saw the scene, she let out a hysterical laugh,
but then immediately muffled her head in her rebozo—she'd
taken to imitating my grandmother's habit of wearing a shawl in
the late afternoon—and stifled her embarrassing laughter. Grandma,
still standing there, started to cry.

I didn't dare ask why. She continued to cry, uncontrolla-
bly. I said to myself, "What's she crying for?" Then the penny
dropped and I answered my own question, "She's crying for me,
for what happened in the bakery." A night watchman had brought
the story to the house. Nothing could stay hidden for long in
Agustini.

"Take her to the bathroom and clean her off!" my grandmother barked at Dulce.

I could still hear my mother weeping in her bedroom. But
"Blowing in the Wind" was also echoing in my inner ear. I had

to make an effort to focus, to sweep away the song, and remember that those men had indeed carried me into the bakery, but immediately I repressed the impact by forcing it into a distant past. It had happened so long ago. It had been horrible, but it didn't have the least connection to now.

At that moment the teacher caught up with me. Somebody had kept him talking at the door of the house, he explained.

"Good evening," he said, breaking in on my grandmother's laments. "So nice to meet you, madam." He reached out his hand and Grandma took it. "Good evening. Forgive me for barging in, but I do need to talk with you two ladies, if you don't mind. My aunt has told me that you're both terribly worried."

Grandma grasped his arm with both her hands. Suddenly she looked very old, much older than her usual self, older even than the teacher's aunt. She clung to him like a sick and exhausted eagle that has been forced to land so as not to collapse in mid-flight. But she controlled her voice enough to shout, "Come here, daughter!" She guided the teacher to the door of the living room, clinging to him, but at the same time stiff and unhesitating. There she let him go and pulled her key chain out from the pocket of her white cotton dress. She opened the door. Mama, once again back to her habitual narcotic gait, had joined them there. The three went inside without shutting the door.

They had barely gotten inside when my grandmother, still in tears, declared, "It would have been better for us if they'd brought her home dead!"

Dulce and I ignored the order to go to the bathroom and listened to their subdued but still audible conversation. The two women were sobbing, while the teacher was explaining in his calm and musical voice that the whole thing had been no more than a scare, that the bakers had come up from their basement, fearful they might drown in the dreadful downpour, and that the novelty of being up at ground level had unbalanced them. It had been my bad luck to be passing at that moment, but he had followed me into the basement, almost at my heels, and certainly there was no cause for concern. As he'd already said, it was just a scare. Nothing had happened, I'd just had to endure a nasty shaking, but he'd put that to rights with a lemon-flavored ice cream, then with a guanabana-flavored one, topped off by a song or two from his record player. They should quit their crying, because really and truly nothing had happened, and they needn't worry because the true story was certain to get around town, and in fact at the very moment his aunt was making sure it did.

"How can we ever thank you?" said one.

"How can we ever thank you?" echoed the other.

"There's nothing to thank me for," he replied. "It was a real pleasure chatting to Delmira. What a bright girl she is! There's nobody like her in this town when it comes to being quick on the uptake or intelligent or well read."

"You've put your finger on the problem," said Grandma, cutting him off abruptly. Not even in circumstances like these would she allow anyone to speak well of me. She came out of the living room and asked Dulce to order up a cake and some guanabana juice from the kitchen to give to the teacher, without troubling to ask him if he wanted them. With a nod of her head she motioned me to come and sit down with them. Now that she had stopped crying, her face had regained its youthfulness, its indeterminate age.

"Wash your hands first" was all she said to me.

The teacher looked for a hundred excuses to turn down the cake, but nothing availed. He had to submit to the heavy, ritual slice of Sacher torte and a huge glass of fruit juice, before leaving with a bundle of Grandma's chocolate slabs as "a present for your aunt," in addition to a fairly big jar of peach jam and a tin full of cookies and almond candies.

He had hardly gotten out the door when Grandma locked up the living room, maybe afraid somebody would steal the silver candlesticks, or the Russian ikon, or her bells from different parts of the world, made of silver or copper or stone, or the enormous jars of chinaware, rocking lazily on their pedestals, or the huge portrait of Saint Sebastian, painted in Puebla at the close of the seventeenth century.

It was already bedtime. The stars were out, crickets were chirruping, the sun had set without our noticing its strident colors. Her shawl around her shoulders, Grandma slid the bar across the door. She settled into her rocking chair. I stretched out in my hammock. Dulce got out the wide-toothed comb and Mama curled up in front of them.

"With all the commotion about the kid," said Mama, "we didn't notice there's been no news from the farm. Do you suppose anything's gone wrong, with all this rain?"

"If the cows didn't manage to fly," Grandma replied, "more than one of them must have been drowned. Any truck trying to get the news here would have gotten bogged down in the mud. The sooner we get a phone installed out there, the sooner we can stop worrying about what's happening, but God knows when that'll be practical."

Then suddenly, as if dead cows had ceased to matter, as if my scare didn't merit the slightest mention, Grandma coolly turned her attention to telling us that day's story.

29

Grandmother's Story

"Today I'm going to tell you how the Protestants tried to persuade the people of Paraíso to abandon the truth of the Catholic faith.

"It turns out that some English folk had come to live in Paraíso. They were involved in exports, at first just fruits, but then timber—not rubber, of course, because this was before the rubber fever broke out, it was while Europeans still thought that rubber was good only for rubbing out pencil marks—and crocodile skins and snake skins and God knows what else. Those people would have sold their mothers if the price was right. Things went so well for them that they bought one cargo boat after another and a whole bunch of launches for getting their products to the port.

"These English folk weren't like normal people. They had a different lifestyle, they believed in a different god, well, they were Protestants. Now before the kid jumps in with her questions—though she knows better than to interrupt her grandmother—let me explain that Protestants were a group of people who had deserted His Holiness the Pope because their king wanted to scrap his marriage for no better reason than his lust, which is—no questions, thank you—certainly not the right way to behave. Our religion doesn't permit divorce, so the Pope said no way. The king, you see, had already gotten rid of seven women without a word to anybody. He'd actually killed some and imprisoned others, just to remove them from sight. And the Pope had turned a blind eye to it all. Till the issue of divorce came up, that is. There was no way the Pope was going to annul a marriage. Not when the wife in question was the sister of the Catholic king of Spain, a flawless individual, a real saint of a man, who cherished the fear of the Lord in his bosom.

"But we were talking about the English in Paraíso, the ones who'd sell the shirts off their backs, smart guys at selling and even smarter at buying things that would bring in a profit. They were followers of the religion invented by their nasty-minded king, and so they had some funny habits. Of course, the people of Paraíso welcomed them quite openly, because there's nobody more welcoming than the people of Tabasco, the word 'welcoming' could have been invented just to describe us, but they drew the line at the idiocies connected with that religion, if you can call that mishmash of Protestant beliefs a religion. Let me make the sign of the cross, to keep myself from contamination. In the name of the Father, and of the Son, and of the Holy Ghost, amen.

"So it turns out that, not content with doing business with a bit of this and a bit of that—they were making money hand over fist, quite shamelessly, putting out of business folks who'd settled here long before their arrival, folks who were old-style Catholics, very devout in their beliefs—this was when my grandfather lost his seven ships, remember I told you that story—anyway, they decided to convert the innocent inhabitants of Paraíso to Protestantism. Why couldn't they have left us in peace, I'd like to know. They'd already gotten everything they wanted— money, ships, power. One of their daughters was engaged to the governor of Vera Cruz. What more could they want? But no, they insisted on converting folks, trying to get them to renounce the protection of the Pope—and even worse—of the Virgin Mary, because they said the Virgin wasn't a virgin, and even if she was, that was no reason to worship her. They were also against praying to the saints. They had no faith in anything. They had hearts of stone.

"So they decided that they'd had enough of living with people who didn't share their beliefs and they got down to wondering how they could make them Protestants. And what do you think they did? Well, one Saturday night, when the moon was full, so that they could see what they were doing—because there wasn't much in the way of streetlighting in Paraíso—it really was a dump of a place, worse than Agustini, a lot worse, in fact, I think there were only six houses there that had balconies—while the town musicians were playing their usual stuff, strumming on guitars and harps, and beating drums and tambourines, they took down all the images in the church. Aided by the powers of evil, they pulled them all down. But the images started walking just like people, virgins and saints alike gathered in the town center. They stepped out of the wood and stucco. With their false eyelashes on their painted little faces, they'd acquired flesh and bones. And they didn't just walk like any ordinary person. No, they were swaying to the rhythm of the local music, dancing shamelessly and encouraging the people of the town to dance with them, and, of course, the people couldn't resist. These women with their long eyelashes and gaudy makeup were teasing the men, though they were still wearing their sacred raiments which the parish priest had blessed dozens of times. They even say that the rosary hanging from the bosom of the Virgin of Montserrat had been blessed personally by the Pope himself, but of course that's a statue that can work miracles.

"But instead of the Protestants getting what they hoped for—they'd imagined that the people of Paraíso would be disgusted and abandon their priest and church and go attend the

Protestant ceremonies in the dreary shack they called a church, a long shed without a hint of style—but instead of that, the next morning, they got their houses stoned and their warehouses burnt to the ground, and they had to get out of Tabasco fast and for good, for they'd proved they were in league with the Devil, and Paraíso had no more use for them.

"So that's the story of the Protestants in Paraíso. Those English folk were sure taught a lesson. The people of these parts don't seem particularly religious, but they do know right from wrong when it comes down to it. Anyway, the English went to Vera Cruz and since what mattered most to them was making money and getting rich the easiest way they could, they were all baptized Catholics in a group ceremony and quit being Protestants to avoid all the problems it caused. And yes, one of their daughters did marry the son of the governor at that time. He'd once been a suitor of my mother. But that story ended right there, because my grandfather, who was a man of real principle, came across him at the Sarlat's workplace doing something so outrageous to an Indian woman that he went straight to the man's father, the governor, and laid a charge against him. But to my grandfather's astonishment, all the governor said was, 'If the bitches were made for that sort of thing, what's it got to do with you Ulloa people? I don't see what you're so upset about.' So my grandfather refused to have the man in the house ever again, because he didn't want to be connected to that vile brood . . ."

Grandma continued with her story, but by now I was sinking into a profound sleep.

30

The Lizards

She came in without any fuss and, halting on the sidewalk in front of the grocery store, removed the basket from her head and put it on the ground. In a singsong voice she called out, "Get your smo-o-oked sea li-i-izards!" She was a handsome woman with two enormous braids dangling across her naked chest. "Fat, ju-u-uicy sea li-i-izards!" She put lots of vigor into the prolonged syllables, her phrasing falling into the musical cadences typical of the poor people of the coast.

The lizards had their snouts poking out of the basket. Their heads had been fastened to sticks that ran the length of their bodies and beyond the end of their tails and were secured inside the basket. The sticks had been used for turning the lizards during the barbecuing process over smoking embers of green wood.

"I ain't got no tama-a-ales today. Today I got the fattest, ju-u-uiciest sea lizards you good folks ever seen." She continued shouting, but her body remained motionless, her huge mouth wide open, and sailing out of it came the musical cries.

Doña Florinda Becerra, the owner of the grocery store, stepped out onto the street, with her old-fashioned weigh scales in her hand, and said, "What's all this about tamales? This Indian woman's never sold us tamales."

The cries continued as if the store owner had not spoken. And as if there had been no Indian woman to speak about, Doña Florinda went back inside her store and perched on her high throne behind the high counter, visible to us all through the high windows of the storefront. But the rest of us stayed there, giving our opinions. Our conclusion was that, as far as we recalled, we'd never seen this woman selling tamales around here, or selling anything for that matter, though it was always possible in the hubbub of a market day she'd escaped our notice. But today was a regular Tuesday, with little of interest going on, so there was nothing to distract us from checking her out from top to toe. On Saturdays we didn't have time to observe every Indian who came into town to sell something, and it was quite possible we'd overlooked her in the hustle and bustle of the market. But that possibility wouldn't stand up for long. All we needed to do was ask any of the guys around town who liked to have sex with these Indian women, regardless of their cleanliness or even their willingness, since they were convinced such women had no sense of shame—well, their naked chests proved that point beyond a doubt—and no inclination to decline a bit of sport. This woman selling lizards was of impressive stature, and handsome with it, blessed with a huge pair of firm, round breasts. Her torso was shapely, her stomach flat and firm. No guy could have missed her. And the guys were all there today, eyeing her lasciviously, particularly the elderly owner of the hardware store, Don Epitacio de las Heras, along with the younger guys whom my classmates dreamed of marrying one day, plus a whole bunch of others, all savoring the sight and pondering what trick or bribe, what act of deceit or violence, would get her into bed with them fast. Dr. Andrade was dreaming, no doubt, that she would approach him in search of medical attention, Don Epitacio hoping she'd come into his store for something she needed, and the crowd of boys figuring that they'd wait for her on the outskirts of town,

wife, and then another, and then a third darted forward to buy her lizard-on-a-stick, till by the end of the day there wasn't a decent household in Agustini that didn't have one or even a pair of them in its kitchen. Though we'd held out for an incredibly long time, by the time the sun went down every housewife in town had finally been seduced by her wares. Only one lizard remained in her basket. Dr. Andrade sent a kid to ask her if she had any aches or pains she needed fixing, because he was available to treat her in his consulting rooms right then and there, letting her know he was an expert in women's ailments, able to guarantee a woman would never have any children she didn't want to. Don Epitacio sent his boys to tell her that if she needed to take home a tool or a padlock or a length of chain, he'd give it to her at a special discount. The gang of youths was already planning to use a car belonging to an uncle to ambush her on the highway. Then suddenly she startled us all by producing from somewhere a wide-brimmed hat and putting it on her head. Where it came from, nobody could say, because we'd had more than enough time to observe everything about her. Maybe it was made of jipijapa, a fiber as delicate as silk that allows a garment to be rolled up so tight it can be passed through the center of a wedding ring. She could have had it wrapped around her waist, inside her skirt. Then she let out a long, fierce whistle that echoed around the town, and went down to the side of the river with its rippling waters.

Her powerful whistle awoke the lizards. It de-smoked them. It untied them. They emerged from the houses, flying grotesquely or creeping or jumping, all heading toward the river. There they plunged in and began to swim, as if they had never been killed and smoked, swimming with the ease of freshwater fish, though they were saltwater creatures. Clinging to her basket, the woman shook her hat, crouching down, almost scraping the ground with the fine material. On the sand, where her bare feet rested, there appeared embers of a fire nobody had kindled. With her right hand she continued fanning the embers and with her left she undid the fastenings of her skirt, letting it slip down into the embers. The fire flared up, as if it were consuming paper. Flames shot up high. We began to detect the stink of burning flesh. Then the woman turned into smoke. The fire vanished into thin air, as did her basket. Only her hat remained behind and nobody dared take a step toward it.

"She was a witch!" the kids called out, breaking the silence.

At the word "witch" the hat began to stir. It floated toward the river in the wake of the lizards. As soon as it reached the water, it started to expand. It grew into a small, well-built boat, like the fishing vessels of the town. On it appeared the witch, showing her white teeth, laughing broadly, her hair perfectly groomed, in spotless, gleaming clothes, in a blouse made of a shiny purple taffeta. She began to row downstream. Nobody could have overtaken her, supposing he wanted to, to get back the money paid for the lizards. The villainous witch left us, sailing away on her hat, surrounded by the silver sheen of the revived sea lizards, whose large scales cast an ironic gleam, as if they formed a bed of rolling coins below the boat.

We phoned our relatives who lived downstream to warn them about the witch who was fraudulently selling sea lizards and heading their way. We were unable to send any warning to the farm. But luckily she didn't go there. She was out to deceive only educated whites. As an Indian, she didn't take advantage of her own sort.

I actually witnessed all these events, but the minute they were over I had difficulty trusting what my senses had perceived. While the events were happening, I couldn't take my eyes off them. Their impact on me was so strong I was intrigued, enthralled, seduced. They had had the power to defy the laws of logic. I mean, how can a smoked sea creature, roasted on a stick, undo its own smoking, take back its own death at the stake? How can fire emerge from hot sand? No hat of jipijapa can transform itself into a boat simply by making contact with water. And yet— I can't help feeling these things did happen, at least to me.

I wasn't scared by what happened. I didn't utter the slightest whimper when she took off, gliding peacefully downstream. I didn't get overexcited when I saw her disappear in a sudden fire that was kindled without fuel. My eyes had certainly witnessed all this, there's nothing false in what I've told you, but for all that I had no faith in it and was determined to believe it hadn't really happened. That afternoon I aligned myself with the liberal rationalism of the teacher. "This is all nonsense, Delmira," he'd told me. "The whites around here are so terrified that one of these days somebody's going to pay them back for all the injuries they've done the Indians. They invent a heap of hogwash as soon as anybody with an ounce of style takes them for a ride. They invest the person with magic powers. Why? So no real-life Indian could do the same thing. But it also shows us how frightened they are of the Indians. And if the Indians one day get it together and turn on the whites, that fear will be well justified. But don't let these idiotic tales occupy even the tiniest corner of your brain."

I'll just say I settled for being a skeptic in these matters. I adopted the teacher's attitude as my own. But even so my wild imagination, conditioned by life in Agustini, still wanted to work overtime. When I came out of my bedroom in the mornings, there wasn't a single day I didn't see a horse flying across the patio or a crowd of Indian women crouched on the ground, sucking on watermelons, and my grandmother trying to drive them away by clapping her hands and saying, "These stinking women, full of fleas! They pestered me when I was a kid, and they're still doing it today, looking exactly the same, still up to their filthy, no-good tricks. I'm an old woman now. What did I do to deserve this?

Why are they still here bugging us, if they don't really exist? Why
are they haunting us?" Or there would be the Indian who sold
gold trinkets, on a swing in front of our eyes, jiggling his wine-
colored bag by its upper rim. "Just give me whatever bill you've
got in your hand and I'll pull out a ring, a tooth, a necklace,
whatever luck brings you. Even a crucifix of solid gold or an
engraved medal." Or a pack of dogs chatting away in the language of Cervantes. Or an albino crocodile they'd brought from
the swamp at the farm. As if it were just an everyday animal, they
let it loose near the fountain in the patio, and it raced off down
the streets of the town, wagging its prodigious tail behind it,
producing panic and leaving a trail of blood in its wake, while its
jaws snapped open and shut, open and shut, controlled by some
deadly, tireless mechanism. In those days, a small animal could
emerge from any flower I walked by. Eggs came out of male
ducks. Insects turned into blossoms. The women who went down
to the river to wash clothes grew terrified of singing after their
songs turned again and again into ugly-looking, ugly-smelling
worms that poisoned the fish for days on end.

   "That's the way things are in this damned town," Grandma
used to say, as she trimmed away from the plants in the patio's
flowerpots the shoots devoured by the latest swarm of bugs. Her
tone was midway between one of exemplary resignation and
unashamed amusement. And it didn't alter, even when one day
she awoke with half her body transformed into that of a hen.
She forestalled the complete transformation by pure force of will,
screaming and hollering loud and long. When we heard her
screams, everybody in the house ran to see what was wrong and
discovered the sorry condition she was in, lying there on her fluttering, floating shawl. Immediately we witnessed her henlike half
disappear, to be replaced by her ordinary self, without a single
trace of the hen remaining. Restored to normal, she adopted the
habit of keeping her shoes on, as if to assert that her feet never

left the ground and that she rejected any idea of floating in midair while she slept.

"Granny," I asked, sincerely concerned for her welfare, "did
you get hurt? Was it painful? Is there anything I can do to help?"

"What do you mean 'Granny'? I've no idea who your
granny is. That's all I need. To be addressed in the diminutive,
as if I was ready for the rest home." What rest home was she
talking about? She must have gotten the term out of a book because there was certainly no rest home in Agustini, or even anything remotely like one. Old folks lived at home, telling stories
to their families, making chocolate and almond candies for them,
old before their time but staying young and active till the day
arrived for them to slip quietly into their graves.

I did let the business about "Granny" slip out in the presence of the teacher, but I took extreme care not to mention
anything about seeing her half-turned into a hen. I didn't mention to him, either, the other things that were happening every
day around town. And he said nothing to me about them. I visited
him frequently, but not a word passed between us about such
things. Taking advantage of the holidays, he was reading avidly,
shut up in his house, so maybe he wasn't aware of what went
on, but I doubt it. His aunt went to the market every day and
she must have known all the latest that was said and done in
Agustini. But maybe, like me, she thought it best not to keep
him up to date on these weird occurrences.

31

The Wonder-working Machine

All the girls my age had cleared out of town. But they were replaced by other girls who had left Agustini two or three years earlier, in order to "study," if we can pervert the term to describe what they'd been up to. They came back loaded with new dresses and new habits picked up at new types of parties. Behind them they dragged boyfriends recruited God knows where, but all of them local boys of the right class, owners of nearby properties, intended to form powerful commercial and financial alliances at the altar. The returning girls held celebrations at which they swapped information and ideas for their upcoming weddings. Then came the wedding ceremonies themselves, and after that the town returned to its normal preoccupation with Christmas parties and the New Year celebrations we held every two or three years.

At these parties it was customary to curse the place we lived in for a hundred good reasons. We dreamed aloud of somehow making it like other places or what we imagined other distant places with gentler climates could be like. To reduce the impact of the heat, we planned to install air-conditioning. We planned to get rid of the hordes of insects, to clear out the "useless" jungle vegetation, or at least dress up the outskirts of the town with a "nice lawn or two, to add a touch of prettiness." We planned ways to escape the intolerable humidity. Pedro Camargo, the doctor's son, a road engineer, had a dream of ridding the town of its "stinking river that is totally useless." He proposed putting the branch of the Grijalva, as the Rio Seco was called where it crossed our town, inside a pipe or getting rid of it altogether by dynamiting its course through the Coletero Gorge, a deep ravine some twenty miles to the south, where its waters came roaring down for thirty of forty feet, creating one of the loveliest landscapes in the region. But others had even bigger ideas. Old Baldy de la Fuente talked a lot about petroleum. He went about explaining how in five years at the most it would make us all richer than rich. People thought he was an idiot and didn't give him the time of day; it was just another mad idea of this weirdo who didn't send his kids to private schools and who, like outsiders, couldn't see anything wrong with the lousy jungle. As well, he was involved with the oil workers and the shady history of their union. He liked to make uncomfortable, even downright scandalous remarks, even though the chief of police was never far behind him, haunting him like a shadow and whispering nastily about him, claiming he was a communist troublemaker and that somebody someday would have to deal with him, to stop him from bringing even more problems to Agustini.

Amalia, Old Baldy's aunt, owned the biggest cocoa plantation in the area, and she had a notorious number of blacks working for her there, since her family had had black workers from way back. "These local Indians are total losers, I can't figure out what they're good for, it's just a waste of time and money to hire them, get yourself some blacks like I do, that's the secret of my family's success." This was her constant patter and Grandma would invariably respond with: "Well, you may be worth a fortune, and the rest of your family too, but if you've got blacks working for you, you'd better have something to plug your noses with because those guys stink to high heaven. And they go banging on drums all night long, swaying their behinds and rousing evil spirits."

One night Amalia turned on Lucho Aguilar, the chief of police, with celestial disdain. "So what's it got to do with you, eh? Why do you keep going on about Old Baldy? What business of yours if he does bring us a few problems? You're not from around here, anyway. You're from Ciudad del Carmen. Ask yourself how you and your relatives got to make yourselves so comfortable here. Baldy won't make any problems for you or your dumb cops. My nephew isn't the sort to go stealing even a single cocoa bean, and he doesn't go sniffing out cunt where he doesn't belong. He's the most decent fellow this goddam town ever laid eyes on. You won't catch him slinking from one bed to another, like some people I could mention. He doesn't go snitching oranges from other people's patios, and he doesn't use paper for anything except to wipe his bum."

Lucho Aguilar was so embarrassed he didn't know what to say. Maybe he didn't realize what Amalia was getting at. He didn't have a woman and didn't seem to be courting one. But it was unthinkable that any bachelor in Agustini wouldn't be out chasing single girls or sneaking off with married ones, so people made up stories about who it was he could be sleeping with. Since he was from out of town, he didn't have his own house or even a relative to live with. Amalia was smart enough to take advantage of that and was renting him a room at the far end of her patio. She was aware that he stole an orange now and then and that he even ate his own boogers without caring who saw him. He was also given to scribbling verses on bits of paper he let nobody see, a needless precaution since his handwriting was said to be illegible. He had a little round face, same as his brothers', thick, dark, curly hair, a tiny clownish nose smack in the center of his face, and a smile which was somewhere between sad and naughty and which made him look more disconcerting than usual. He was known variously as Lucho or the Big Dummy or as a smart-ass schemer, whose cold head was constantly coming up with unlikely schemes not worth worrying over.

It was unusual for the men and women at our parties to get involved in a lengthy conversation. We preferred short, snappy exchanges, often suggestive or aggressive. When men got together without their womenfolk, the talk turned to money or business. The women's regular topics were clothes, hairdos, the latest furniture they'd bought for their houses, the endless failings of those idle Indians, who were responsible for everything wrong with the country, and how they'd just love to leave Agustini and go live in a decent city where you didn't find snakes in your cooking vessels and where witches and ghosts didn't appear in the town square at the slightest provocation.

Every party required a good number of servants, not counting those involved in cooking the food. They removed dirty plates, glasses, and ashtrays, they filled wineglasses, at the door they checked in hats, shawls, handbags, raincoats, they marshaled the arriving cars so that the guests could get out right at the door of the house without getting their dress shoes of patent leather or shiny silk befouled with mud. A wall of servants existed to make sure nothing or nobody untoward entered the celebrations from outside. Inside, order was guaranteed. Parties and weddings followed a rigid routine that never varied. Strangers from out of town, the grooms and brides-to-be of our young people, their families and friends, neighbors from upriver and downriver, the owners of farms in the highlands, all accepted the status quo. If an army of Indians sucking watermelons had shown up to bother us the way they bothered my grandmother as a child, the wall of servants would have repelled them. If a beautiful witch had tried to walk naked across the patio where the partygoers were assembled, the wall would have barred her passage too. If a cloud of oranges had come floating down here, the wall would have screened it out like unwanted insects. If some bizarre flying snake had wafted this way, the wall would have sprouted blazing torches to repel it. At these parties nothing outrageous was allowed entrance. Everything was chic, just as it should be. An air of elegance had to be maintained, tricked out with the modest novelties the returning girls had brought with them. Novelties like drinking store-bought soda pop, wearing clothes from the USA, or smoking cigarettes rolled by machine, not rolled between palm and thigh like the cigars from the store of the Spanish-born Don Emilio, who had arranged for *Anna Karenina* or *War and Peace* to be read aloud during the process. Don Emilio had substituted Tolstoy forty years previously, declaring, "There's no way I'm going to have the bolshy blacks in my factory listening to the stupidities of *Don Quixote* or Quevedo's *Petty Thief*. You've seen what problems all that reading caused in Spain."

All my peers had now left Agustini for Puebla, Mérida, Villahermosa, Mexico City, or Switzerland. The granddaughters of the wealthy, paralyzed furniture dealer had gone to spend a year in French-speaking Switzerland. I had been left behind. By now I was a pretty young thing, so I got invitations to all the parties. I didn't want to go, but my grandmother almost literally dragged me to them.

Kids and magical events were forcibly expelled from these parties, but that didn't give me an out. I was forced to attend them because of my family's obstinacy. According to my grandmother, I was being "buried alive in this shitty town," stuck here because she'd been soft enough to listen to the priest and the teacher, but even so, she wasn't going to see me disappear from decent society. Decent society? It took all my resources to escape the chubby paw of Marilyn's father, always on the lookout for a chance to pinch my bum when nobody was watching. He was spurred on by my innovative style of dressing (of which more later) and by the rumors that had been spread about me after the incident at the bakery. The gossip had taken on new life after my mother and grandmother had yielded to the pressure from the priest to let me complete my secondary education at a public school, an education hardly fitting for a girl destined for marriage. Even so, it wasn't necessary to let my imagination run wild to add excitement to these parties. There were enough natural excesses around without that. A wedding was all that was needed to get the ladies decked out, fur stoles on their shoulders and necklaces of diamonds and rubies over evening dresses that cost hundreds and hundreds of dollars. The Indians peered at these garments from the shadows, unable to understand what metals were woven into the gauze or lamé fabrics and into the chokers decorated with appliqués. They never could have imagined even for a moment that it was thanks to their underpaid labor that the whites were able to lavish such luxuries on themselves.

Brides traveled from the church to the site of the reception in flashy Cadillacs brought to Agustini especially for the purpose. There was competition to see who could spend the most on food and bands and dances and dresses. The centers of the tables were adorned with paper or plastic flowers, with out-of-season fruits and plants raised in greenhouses; orchids ravished from the depths of the forest and giving off dark, disconcerting odors were paraded on the chests of our princesses, along with sentimental verses, a pearl, a feather, and vile-smelling exotic leaves, shanghaied in some dusky dell in order to wilt far from home as part of a gaudy corsage reeking of jungle decay.

For all this, I did get to know a woman who did me some genuine favors. She was a sly wheeler-dealer from the north of Mexico who brought in clothes from the United States. She traveled the whole country at a dizzying pace, toting with her the many brands of merchandise her varied clientele demanded. Other girls went for her pink dresses and her stuffy, provincial, ladylike jackets with their ever-so-daring gilded buttons, but backed up by the wallet of my uncle Gustavo, ever accessible to his niece, I ordered items in the latest fashion and was the first to introduce into Agustini the miniskirt, the belt with a massive buckle fastening over the hip, striped stockings that went well with a tight-fitting blouse, dresses made of paper with a psychedelic design, packed in a box of the same design, and pants in startlingly bright colors that ended as tight as tubes on the calves.

For one wedding my former classmates had returned from their boarding schools in Puebla and at parties wore long, misty dresses, the bodices tarted up with fake jewels, with brooches adorning the bases of long, sumptuous trains, giving them the appearance of outlandish fowls. In contrast, I had ordered in a dress of pleated material, attached to a silvery, slender choker. It had no shoulders—which in itself was enough to cause a sensation—and it ended two inches above the knee—a second sensation, heralding moral turbulence—together with silvered shoes with an unusually big buckle and wide heels that produced as much impact as all the rest of my outfit put together. I put my hair up in a ponytail, as high up on my head as it would go, and refused to back-comb it or put it in curlers. But I did use lots of spray, which drenched my hair, as well as Dulce and me, because she'd be combing my hair while I gave her instructions, in enough icky goo to set it totally rigid, like a doll's.

My grandmother was outraged by my appearance. "Have you any idea what you look like!" she kept on saying. "Where did this girl come from? Wherever did she get such ideas?"

My anguished mother would add, "Get rid of those vile colors. They're an eyesore. You shouldn't let her go out like that, Mama, with her legs showing. What will the men in town say? I mean, what kind of man will want to marry a girl who parades around flashing her thighs, like somebody who's no better than she should be. I've never seen anything like it around here. Even sluts dress with more discretion."

But my usually officious grandmother had stopped listening. Her horror at my style of dressing had by now rendered her indifferent to the outrageous shortness of my skirt. Her eyes refused to see anything below my waist; her ears declined to grasp what my mother was saying.

But it didn't take long for my mother to find a way to check my spending on clothes. When the wedding season was over, one evening when Grandma was about to start her nightly story, Mama presented her with the final bill of my supplier, determined to convince her not to let Gustavo go on throwing money away on my bizarre outfits. Grandma listened to her arguments, which tactfully omitted all mention of my bare thighs, and agreed with her. That conversation blocked my access to Gustavo's wallet. I replied it was Gustavo's money they were talking about, that he'd okayed my spending it on whatever clothes I chose, but Grandma came at me with "In this house I give the orders!" She was right. The final yes or no was always hers.

School classes were scheduled to get under way the coming week. The dealer had my latest order ready, a bundle of oddities in the latest U.S. style, which I planned to wear at the secondary school. "No way!" said Grandmother. I'd received permission to buy a "discreet" outfit. "And no fancy colors," added my grandmother, supplemented by "and nothing indecent" from my mother. Just one outfit and nothing more. "Buy something that will go with what you've already got, something that won't call too much attention to itself. Look, something like this." She delayed doing her accounts to make her point. "Put on a beige skirt and you can wear it with the brown blouse or the silk sand-colored blouse, the one Gustavo brought you. You could get yourself as well . . . " Dulce realized that this hymn in honor of discretion in dress was going to replace the nightly story and she started the ritual combing. Meanwhile I managed to turn my mind to other things as Grandmother blah-blah'ed on, and eventually I fell asleep.

The next day I bought from my convention-flouting dealer a pair of jeans and a white, long-sleeved shirt that was to bring a disgusted protest from my grandmother. "Looks like a man's!" she declared, all vitreous gaze and imperious tone. But to the rest of the dealer's merchandise I was obliged to say a regretful no. "Don't fret yourself," she said, when she saw my worried face. "There are plenty of gals in Mexico City only too glad to buy this stuff. It's all so fashionable." I'd planned to borrow one of Uncle Gustavo's ties from his wardrobe, as soon as I got a chance to talk to him by phone or see him on one of his flying visits. A tie would add a final touch of scandalous modernity to my getup. My darling uncle was my delighted accomplice in whatever scheme I came up with, because he realized that in my heart of hearts I intended no malice. At that time of my life I was an angel. I say it in full seriousness. All I wanted was to find the quickest way to bring peace and prosperity to the whole of mankind.

problems, really had to study history, really had to read aloud in front of the class. You had to write précis without spelling errors and take tests in comprehension. It turned out I knew less about the history of Mexico and the rest of the world than other students my age. What was the date of the Fall of Constantinople? When had Jerusalem fallen into the hands of the Saracens? At what date did Christianity become the official religion of the Roman Empire? These were a sample of the questions I couldn't answer. The nuns had highlighted key events in the history of the Catholic Church and reduced the history of the world to it. According to them, there were no other religions, no other cultures, no other latitudes but our own. Although I lived barely two miles from the only brick-built pyramids in Meso-America, although our region had been the headquarters of the great Olmec artists and a highway to the Mayas, the nuns never once mentioned the names of the Olmecs and Mayas, not in my hearing anyway. I knew of the existence of the emperor Maximilian because the nuns had a soft spot for him. I'd heard of Porfirio Díaz and Iturbide for the same reason. But the name of Benito Juárez, a name often spoken at my new school, had never been mentioned, not even briefly, at the convent school. Not even in a passing whisper. For the nuns there had been no such person as Hidalgo, the shady priest who had acted as architect of Mexican independence from Spain. There were no rebel leaders like Morelos or Guerrero or Pancho Villa. The French Revolution had never taken place. The history of the world was synonymous with that of the Catholic Church, and that itself had been thoroughly sanitized. The nuns censored themselves without realizing it, feeling more secure, the greater their ignorance of the world at large, stupid maybe but with stony fortitude all the stronger for its stupidity. At the secondary school I first heard Hitler's name and that of Luther spoken outside of a context of religious scandal. The nuns bracketed both together as the chief enemies of all that was good, along with Emiliano Zapata. But I'd no idea who lived when.

By and large the students were of mixed race. We even had among us a pair of pure Indians who came in daily from the outlying farms. What we didn't have was what my grandmother would call "nice people." Not a single girl from the "decent" families in town. And among the boys only the son of Old Baldy de la Fuente. But he was a lost cause, anyway, who'd abandoned all claim to be considered "nice." He was no longer "one of us," though he still attended nice people's parties and in church occupied the pew his family had purchased. I now shared a desk with the kind of people who, on Sunday nights, didn't circulate around the bandstand but sat on the sidelines, looking on, who heard Mass standing at the back of the nave, or who went to the eight o'clock Mass. People, in short, I'd never mixed with before.

At break time I checked out the students around me on a score of issues. Some had the same dreams as I. Others had been infected by a new disease whose impact I still hadn't managed to appreciate fully: the black-gold fever which had lately hit the area. That was why, they explained to me, they were clearing vast sections of jungle. Only a stick-in-the-mud would clear land to pasture herds of cattle on it or to bring in the hump-backed cows which were resistant to the heat and to most tropical fevers. Those who were wide-awake had sniffed out where the big money really was. Granted the petroleum belonged to the state and couldn't be considered anyone's private property, but the coming prosperity would be more than enough to rescue the country from its economic doldrums as well as fill the pockets of well drillers, technicians, and marketers. It was to be the salvation of Mexico. But it was news to me. And though the news might be true, it meant nothing much to people of my social class. My new acquaintances kept talking about Mexico. People like my family didn't give a damn about Mexico.

The son of Old Baldy, who was nicknamed "Young Baldy," kept talking about the Petroleum Workers Union and Socialism. I immediately learned that his father had paid several visits to Cuba and I picked up some idea of the wild kinds of things going on there. Until then I'd never heard mention of the Cuban Revolution. I also realized that Cuba had been erased from the wall map hanging in the convent school. Once the wealthy families of Agustini had bought their dresses and angled for husbands in Havana, but now, thanks to its uncomfortable social experiment, it had been eliminated from the globe. In Young Baldy's house there hung on the wall a framed photograph of Old Baldy with Fidel Castro.

Each day Young Baldy would play his guitar. Once classes were over, he'd settle himself on the patio, under the basketball hoop, with his instrument and chant Latin American songs that were new to me. All the other students joined in the choruses: "Give birth, give birth, mothers of Latin America, to a young guerrilla" or "Lend a hand to the Indian and you'll be doing good." My instinctual choice to wear a blouse and jeans meant that I'd done the perfect thing to make me part of this clan. Suddenly I saw myself at the heart of a new, attractive family. I had around me people I could tell my troubles to. I could share ideas with them, in a way I'd never been able to do in my own home. I had a father in the person of the teacher, a father who was young and generous, full of life and sprightly chatter, who was out to turn us all into heroic saviors of the world and who, as a final blessing, had a record player, newspapers and magazines, and who knew everything that was going on in the world. I could have found no better guide to the dreams of the sixties.

33

World Map

As soon as my mind was able to put together a sketchy map of the world, with the countries more or less where they should be—a map that did not fit well with the nuns' version of the world, one sponsored by Agustini and the Vatican and passed off as the only possible reality—I began to spin threads from one place to another, making connections like a busy spider.

Some of the connections broke the second I made them. I struggled to build a tie between Copenhagen and Villahermosa, though I can't say exactly why. I suppose it had something to do with a desire to span the distance between what my childhood reading had spawned in my imagination and the daily reality I was living. I was too far from the land of the "Little Mermaid" and Hans Andersen for the connection to hold. The tie snapped. Maybe if I'd summoned the aid of Karen Blixen, I'd have done better. I suspect she would have readily approved of the efforts of a gauche adolescent to connect a jungle region, home to flamingos and crocodiles, with the frost-bound peace of her country. If the spirit of Isak Dinesen had stretched out a hand in answer to my plea, the bond would have held in spite of its local changes, just like the phone cables which were coming to Agustini did, though loaded down with birds' nests, bromeliads, and lianas, their poles infested with green life, converted into vegetation. But I didn't call on Dinesen. The first thread I spun got warped and came drifting down with the first change in the weather. So I turned to imitating Hamlet, attempting to recover my lost father, who had been eliminated by the women in my home with the ruthlessness Gertrude showed to Hamlet's father.

Over time I had collected some information from my kindly teacher: my father was living in London, teaching at the university. He was a close friend of Gustavo, with whom he had studied in Italy, where my father came from. But he had abandoned his native country altogether, while Gustavo had returned to the capital of his. Papa had broken with Mama early on in their relations. My grandmother loathed him, principally because she didn't know what to make of him. "He's so different from the folks in Agustini. He's not like anybody else." But he hadn't married again. I stretched a thread from London to Agustini. What a ridiculous name "Agustini" was! I suppose the only reason to call it that was to emphasize that it hadn't been founded by the Indians, like neighboring Comalcalco, Cunduacan, Huimanguillo, Tenosique, Macuspana, Nacajuna, or Tacotalpa. I pulled out the thread carefully so as not to overstrain it, so that it could support the humming transit of my thoughts from one end of it to the other.

After I discovered Kafka, another debt I owe to my teacher, I stretched a line from my hometown to Prague. I then said goodbye to London and it was to Prague, to its terrible castle and handsome bridges and inviting alleyways, that I longed to go. I tightened the connection that I'd first left tentative, and it held. I made the connection even tighter, dreaming absurd dreams of going there as soon as I got the chance. I gathered my dreams together with the tireless patience I had seen modeled in the obsessive embroidering of the nuns. Prague had what it took to keep me fascinated. Not only did it offer the finest works of literature, not only did it enjoy a compelling beauty I had admired in Gustavo's encyclopedias, but it belonged to a world with a different structure than mine, distinct from the one I knew, a socialist, well, a communist world, where by now everybody would be sure to have learned—so I told myself—to live as equals, where a new morality had been set in place, radically at odds with that of Agustini. I recall the shock I got one day at the beauty salon, where I'd gone for a trim, when I picked up a copy of *Reader's Digest* and read an article about the hundreds of East Germans who risked life and limb to escape into the capitalist sector of Berlin. It had to be puerile Yankee propaganda. One more of the lies of capitalism. I read the piece with intense anxiety, I checked over the accounts of witnesses several times. Finally I consulted the teacher on the truth of it all. "I just don't get what they could be thinking of!" I still said to myself. "Are they crazy or what?" Because at that time I'd have risked my own life to flee in the opposite direction, to escape from Agustini to Prague. So strong, so overstrong was the bond I'd forged just then between my city and that of Kafka.

But I soon went back to my link with London. In no time at all I was visiting it again in my imagination. It was the place for me. There lived the Rolling Stones, my father, and Twiggy, and in my jumbled understanding, they all met in Carnaby Street, rubbing shoulders with Joseph Conrad, the author of my beloved *The Secret Agent,* while Sherlock Holmes, Dickens, Wilkie Collins, and the Beatles strolled by.

The attraction of my London lay in the endless possibilities which gave it zestful new depths and a certain high-toned style. In Agustini, daily life licensed droll kinks and pious follies, but none of them was profound enough to stir the lower depths of its smugness. Underneath the screwy surfaces, events retained a grating sameness. People could fly, birds could plummet from the skies, but the social structure stayed intact. I was an Ulloa and I could swerve and pivot and dive forever, but I would always come up as an Ulloa. Just as Dulce would always be a nanny, and the boy who smelled of pee would never smell of anything different.

Once the bond that tied Agustini to London was snugly in place, I felt myself within striking distance of England, a promised land where I'd find both common sense and a freedom to nourish my fantasies and make them come true. There glowed my world of tomorrow. There young people were pulling down social institutions, shaking the establishment to its foundations, and in its place erecting a paradise of egalitarian dreams. But my fantasies lacked stamina and precision, fed only by their own fuzziness. The sole certainty that lasted for more than a brief while was the knowledge that I had to get out of Agustini. My time was up. I had to find another place to go if I was to keep on living. My miniskirts and I, my hopes for a more just world, my unspoken daydreams—we had to get away, find somewhere else to mint the new currency of our dreams.

Like anybody who discovers that the world is a lot bigger than she previously imagined, I wanted to leave my footprints across its newly discovered vastness and make it all mine. I couldn't bear to know that the planet had so much length and breadth to offer me, and sit tight. I had to enter the larger world. I had to gobble up its distances. I had to feed right and left on what it had to offer. Driven by God knows what spiritual inheritance, I had to explore it all, a conquistador in a miniskirt.

But the desire that consumed my breast, more than a passion to travel and a hope of creating a better world, was the desire to become a writer. I was already, I assured myself, something of a writer, because I was so different from all those around me at home. And it didn't take me long to see I was also different from those in my school. Social class, academic class, I was a loner. The advantage of jamming three grades into a single classroom was that a smart student who cared to eavesdrop could complete three years' work in two. I finished my junior high education with good grades a year early, and the next step was to move to Mexico City, where I would finish senior high school and enter the university. At least that was the plan of Gustavo and my teacher. But it wasn't what I had in mind. I wanted to cross the ocean, get to know other latitudes. I'd just discovered that the world was round, that Agustini was not the center of the universe, and I wanted to take full advantage of that knowledge. I had to escape, to travel, to see other horizons. I planned to live a grand variety of adventures in India, New Zealand, London, Sri Lanka, Prague, South Africa. Then I'd settle down and write my books. I had even decided exactly what it was I'd write. My magnum opus was to be a voluminous novel in which the characters revealed their personalities only by the way they walked. There was no plot, no anecdotes, no interaction, no narrative complication whatever. My characters walked from page to page and their gaits revealed their souls. My book, I can see now, was to be like a German herbology, with pictures of leaves and flowers of the itemized plant on each page. I would sketch in words the style and force of my characters' movements, and my characters would number hundreds, even thousands, possibly encompass every person who lived in Agustini, all of them condemned to walk through my uncountable pages, strutting or sidling, strolling or striding, dragging their feet or swinging their arms, parading stiffly or rolling their hips, floppy and flaccid or rigid from head to toe. The opening lines of the book were to be: "If you creep, you walk. If you fly, you walk. If you jump, you walk. Whether you are man or woman, you walk. If you are a child, you walk. If you are somebody's dog, you walk. If you are somebody's lord and master, you walk. So walk on by, and I will paint your gait in words."

I began to pile up notes in exercise books, on scraps of paper, in my head. Nobody, I knew, had ever done this before. I saw

1967

34

They Killed Old Baldy

One afternoon a bunch of gossips came to tell us that Old Baldy de la Fuente had been killed. It had happened on the highway. The car he'd been driving had been forced off the road. Then they put two bullets into him, so that nobody would mistake his death for an accident. While the gossips passed on the news, Young Baldy was strumming away on his guitar, practicing the chords for "We Shall Overcome." Suddenly he realized what they were saying. He had built a protective fence around himself with his nonstop music, but their words finally penetrated it. And while the women were going over the details for the third or fourth time, he threw down his instrument, bellowing crazily, "It isn't true, it isn't true!" The teacher placed a firm hand on his shoulder and said, "Be strong, Young Baldy. It is true." But the more the teacher said so, the louder Young Baldy screamed it wasn't, but without shedding a single tear.

The teacher's aunt marched out of the kitchen, where she invariably made us sandwiches, dry-eyed also, and the group of gossips followed her into the sitting room. The door to the street had been left open and neighbors were gathering outside. Some came in, in the wake of the gossips, while others left to be replaced by others arriving from the market. They poked their heads

and shoulders around the door, watching to see when Young
Baldy would snap.

"Is everybody heartless in this town?" asked the aunt in her
high-pitched, schoolmistressy voice. "Ladies, you don't give
people this sort of news in that way. Excuse me." She took one
of the women by the elbow and shepherded her to the door,
and the rest of the sheep followed close behind. "Can't you see
the man's son is here? Is it too much to expect you to show a bit
of tact? Really, I've never seen anything like it! Go to the church
and pray for the man's soul. Give his relatives a chance to deal
with their terrible grief. Out of here, all of you! Really, the lack
of consideration . . ."

The women had fallen silent and the aunt shut the door
behind them. Young Baldy, trembling from head to foot, was
still shouting, "It's not possible!" The teacher still held him by
the shoulder.

"Don't you have any feelings, either?" the aunt barked at
her nephew in a tone that was both angry and surprised. She
pulled his hand away from the boy's shoulder. "Come here,
Young Baldy, my dear. Come and cry with me."

She hugged him tight. The skinny body of Young Baldy
lost all its force and he crumbled in her arms. She drew him over
to the armchair and sat him on her lap. He started to cry, clinging to her neck, his face hidden on her chest, while she stroked
his head and shoulders, crying herself now.

"My poor Young Baldy," she was saying. "How could those
miserable types do this to my poor Young Baldy?"

The boy arched his back, almost in a convulsion, letting
out howls that were broken by "Papa, Papa." He slumped down
to the floor and rested his head in defeat on her knees, one hand
drooping from the chair and rubbing against the cement floor.
You might have been tempted to think that the strengthless body

of Young Baldy himself, supported by the aunt's arms, was that of the dead man.

By the time the priest arrived, they had assumed the posture of Michelangelo's Pietà. We clustered around them, mourning, buried in grief. Except for the teacher. His cheeks were totally dry. The priest, pronouncing staunch words of comfort, knelt down in front of the Pietà and started to recite the "Our Father," and everyone but the teacher joined in. More people had gathered outside the house, beside the first group of inquisitive neighbors and the gossips who had brought the bad news, and when they heard us praying, they joined in too. "Thy will be done," we were saying when the teacher abruptly stormed out of the door, pushing his way through the praying people, leaving the metal door ajar. The gossips and their crowd, kids, neighbors, Indians, people coming and going in the direction of the market, had all knelt down in the street. They were crying too as we said three "Our Father"s in a row.

"Young Baldy," said the priest, "we should go see your mother. She needs you. You've got to be strong. You are the man of the house now. Come with me. Let's go."

The mother figure of the Pietà remained where she was, her lap a gaping space, while the Christ figure passed through the mourners and the rest of the crowd that blocked his way. They did not raise their heads as he went but began yet another "Our Father." I and the other friends of Young Baldy went to look for the teacher. We found him sitting under the porticos, staring pensively at a glass of water.

35

The Fly

Holding a trembling glass of water the waiters had placed in front of him to calm him down, but unable to set it down on the wooden surface of the table, the teacher brooded over the fate of Old Baldy. "So they went and killed him, eh? It doesn't take much imagination to realize who did it. We all know who wanted to get rid of him. The ones who tried to bribe him, the ones who offered him a house in Acapulco, who brought a Mercedes-Benz to his front door, who sent him the notorious baskets of goodies every Christmas."

A messenger brought them all the way from Tampico, but Old Baldy was never willing to accept them.

"The engineer has sent you guys this."

"Well, tell him thanks, but no thanks. We don't take gifts at this house. We don't approve of them."

"That's what they told me you'd say, but I gotta leave 'em anyway. I'm not gonna take 'em back with me. Come on, you guys. Don't be like that."

"There's no way we can take them. How about you? Want a glass of guanabana pop?"

The messenger would accept the pop and ended up leaving the basket in the middle of the public park. People would pull out a can of God knows what imported garbage, others walked off with a bottle of champagne, somebody else some Spanish wine, while others grabbed sugared almonds, or candies and dried fruits, or brandy and nuts. These people were all "nice," either businessmen or professionals, because no Indian would have dared touch the basket. Only those in the know, only the respectable folk, would help themselves, for they ran no risk of being accused of theft. Who was going to level a charge against the spotless reputation of Dr. Camargo? Or against Don Epitacio de las Heras, whose honor was as unquestioned as the quality of his locks and chains, or against Florinda Becerra, as far above reproach as the ham, jam, and jugs she sold, a woman as hard as a coin. Or against the prosperous owners of enormous farms, some of the best-established names in Mexico City, who came to Agustini around Christmastime, to visit their mothers and loyal younger brothers who hung on to their properties tooth and nail. Last Christmas, though, there'd been a difference. The engineer had learned what had happened to his baskets, that they were looted by people of no use to him. Not that they were shy about what they did. They would even thank him for what he'd sent. "Fabulous champagne, old man!" and "Next time you're in Agustini, drop by for a glass of the great brandy you were kind enough to give us." So he had sent one of his gun-toting henchmen, who forced the wife of Old Baldy to accept the basket at gunpoint. And it was more grand and more varied than normal, with a complete leg of smoked ham, three big cans of foie gras, several bottles of wine, three of champagne, two more of brandy, canned clams, candies, chocolates, and more.

His eyes still fixed on the glass of water, the teacher experienced an internal explosion. Rage consumed him. Rage devoured him. Swallowed by rage, he kicked and twisted to find his way past it. Up his spine raced a sharp, stinging pain and his arms and legs quivered with its intensity. His skin burned as if boiling oil had been splashed on it, as if the oil had been spooned into his mouth and he had been forced to swallow it, retching at the same time. As he suffered these inner agonies, all the time he was staring fixedly at the glass of water. His hands were now together under the point of his chin, supporting his head, his elbows on the tabletop. He was holding himself rigid, as if to keep the sense of decency upright in the topsy-turvy life of Agustini. Trying to douse the fire that raged inside of him, he swallowed the glass of cool water and dropped it back, spinning, onto the tabletop.

Nothing would ever be the same for the teacher. Old Baldy was dead, a curse had come upon him as Old Baldy fell, nobody could put things back together again. A sense of doom had possessed him. The cool, pure air that had once been full of beating wings, with which he had refreshed his students, was polluted by whirling sand and ashes. The vomit of a volcanic rage had spilled over the land. His tongue seemed to thicken with obscenities, wounding his own palate, poisoning his saliva.

A large black fly, an inch-long bug of buzzing blackness, the sort that haunted stables, landed in the teacher's glass. It made him even more furious. "So now they're throwing flies at me! They don't know who they're dealing with!" The fly stubbornly dived headfirst to the bottom of the glass. Seen through the water and the glass, it appeared immense, twice its regular size.

While rage was consuming the teacher from his trousers to the last button of his shirt, racing through his balls, his guts, his heart, the priest had taken Young Baldy home to his mother. He left them alone and then ran to the church to set the church bells pealing out the death. But the more the bells rang out, the stronger grew the rage inside the teacher, suffocating him. Finally he jumped up, flinging his hands apart. He grabbed the chair and tossed it behind him, exclaiming, "To work!"

This was his slogan. We were used to hearing it in school. It was then he realized we were standing nearby. With an uncanny look, his face ruddy, he said to us, "We've got to get to work at once. Come on. Let's go to the school. We're going to organize a demonstration for this weekend. We've got to let everybody know. Nobody in Agustini will have ever seen anything like it. Yes, that's what we're going to do. It'll be a party like no other. You'll see!"

He babbled on, sometimes incomprehensibly. But he converted our shock and grief into something active, into something close to triumph, the way a huckster can fool us with a pleasing trick and we feel grateful even though we know we're being fooled.

"If this monstrosity had to happen," he went on, "we're not going to let it go to waste. Right now we're going to make sure people everywhere know about it. They're going to know why Old Baldy died and what he was fighting for. If it was somebody else they'd killed, he'd have done the same for them. First, we're going to call his relatives, then we're going to call our own. Wait for me at the school. I'm going to tell the priest." We stood stock-still, unable to obey his order. We couldn't move without him. We had been infected by his rage, but we didn't know what he expected of us. "Okay," he added, understanding, "come along with me and stop looking at me that way."

The priest's house was locked shut. We went looking for him in the church. The nave was empty. In the sacristy we found only one of his faithful altar boys, a six-year-old, dark-skinned and typical of Agustini's poor. The priest fed him daily in return for his sweeping what had already been swept and for his organizing the candles, which came already organized in cardboard boxes, into other cardboard boxes. He also had to fold the clean dusting rags of the nuns and count up all the pennies that had been left in the alms boxes, separating them from the other coins, hoping that there'd be enough of them to make his work worthwhile.

"Where is Father Lima?" the teacher asked him.

"He gone to de bells."

We went into the bell tower. The priest had stripped off his soutane and was sweating heavily. He was hanging on to the bell's rope, clinging to it with legs clad in tight pants, swinging on the rope, his face bathed in tears. As on that terrible day when I discovered him frolicking with my mother, he had discarded his glasses and his face was twisted out of shape, but at that particular moment I did not remark on the similarity. The sound of the rocking bells was deafening. The half-naked priest had his eyes shut and did not see us. As the others called out to him, I ran up the spiral staircase, getting ever closer to the deafening bells, until I reached the top of the tower. I stepped out toward the railing. On it were dangling the priest's glasses. Down below me stretched the panorama of Agustini, and surrounding it, the jungle that threatened to devour us. Resisting the memory of the priest in the hammock with my mother, repressing its sights and sounds, I focused on surveying my town. There lay the public park, below the verdant treetops, there the market, the public school, the convent school next to the convent itself, the nuns' garden, the priest's house, my own house (I'd never realized they were so close), and beyond, the ruins of what had been the lepers' hospital, the highway. If I strained my eyes, I could see on the southern outskirts one of Uncle Gustavo's dreams, the Ferris wheel, half covered by foliage. I put on the priest's glasses. They brought everything closer, tinier, right up to my face.

Chacho touched me on the back. He signaled to me to go down. I followed him down the tower, my vision unreliable because I was still wearing the priest's glasses. At the foot of the stairs, Carlos, another of the students, was now ringing the bells.

I followed Chacho into the sacristy. The priest and the teacher were involved in an intense discussion. The priest had donned his black soutane once more. I took off the glasses and gave them to him. They quickly brought me up to date. "The bells will keep on ringing. We are arranging for people to ring them from one hour to the next. Put your name on the rota. We're organizing groups to look after the rest of the things we've got to do."

36

Old Baldy's Body

When Old Baldy's body arrived in Agustini, the bells were still pealing. It came to the wake surrounded by a mass of mourners. The whole town, summoned by the bells, gathered around the corpse with the solidarity of a family. Everybody was carrying flowers.

The priest received the body at Old Baldy's house, said a blessing over it, and then went off to the bedroom, while others wrapped it in its shroud. He had taken from the shirt pocket of the corpse a small book of phone numbers that Old Baldy always had on him. Some of the pages were stained with blood, but the plastic covers had kept others clean. As the priest was going out, the coffin was being brought in, and he had to jump over a wall of flowers that the mourners had erected in the doorway. He suggested that they leave a way through. And his suggestion worked out well, for they then started to pile up the flowers in front of the house until they covered the whole facade, building a wall of flowers to protect the family's grief.

The whole town filed past, adding their contributions to the wall of flowers. They took their leave of Old Baldy, expressed their condolences to his relatives, to his mother who had made the journey from Villahermosa, to his two sisters recently arrived from Ciudad del Carmen, to Young Baldy and his mother. The teacher and the priest outdid themselves in their efforts to get everything organized. While the church bells kept up their pealing, the priest busied himself phoning people to tell them of Old Baldy's death and inviting them to the funeral, to both the religious ceremony and the civil ceremony that was to follow. He called Villahermosa, the capital, and then Tampico. He called every legible name in Old Baldy's address book, dialing one number after another and explaining who he was. He didn't spare the widow's feelings; he told her what he was doing and asked her and her son to supply the numbers that were unreadable. She had the presence of mind to remember even more names that ought to be called, and suggested that the priest also inform the press. Back then it was not possible to speak long distance by dialing directly. The girl at the switchboard was going out of her mind, for the office she worked in was tiny and she couldn't have the fan running at the same time as she was connecting calls because it somehow produced static on the line. It was already getting dark and it was almost time to close her office for the day when the priest showed up at her door.

"I've come to ask you if you'll put in a few hours' overtime for Old Baldy's sake."

The girl looked dreadfully ill. She had spent hours cooped up in that airless hole, cooking away under the huge blades of the fan she couldn't switch on. She hadn't been able to complete even one line of her usual crocheting. It was normal for her to relax in the breeze of the fan, using her fingers more on her knitting than on making switchboard connections.

"Well, yes, of course. Whatever you say," she replied.

"But first come and get a bite to eat. You look awful."

He took her to the porticos and, sitting down beside her, ordered food and drink. He asked the waiter to give him two of the cardboard fans they used for advertising. They were oval-shaped, of stiff paper, and on one side it said: "Refreshments and ice cream. La Celestina, the best place in Agustini. You'll find it on the east side of the porticos, right next to the church. You can also make phone calls from there [a blatant lie] and buy your lucky lottery tickets too." On the other side was a picture of an Eskimo cuddling a white polar bear, under a northern sky, surrounded by ice which had an inexplicable reddish hue to it. They could be used as fans, because on the side that advertised the business there was glued a small piece of wood, the size of a lollipop stick.

They went back to the switchboard office and spent a couple of hours there, calling long distance and fanning themselves with the advertising material of La Celestina. It got dark and they called it a day. But before he left, the priest gave her a strange blessing in return for her loyal service. "May you live a thousand years and have lots of children. May you be happy in return for your kindness today. May Almighty God give you what you deserve for this day's work."

He didn't promise her a good seat in heaven or a soul free from sin, but only the earthly blessings he believed she deserved for putting up with the heat and making the connections with such perseverance, quarreling with other operators elsewhere and battling with faulty lines. She thanked him for his blessing which sounded delightful to her ears. She was a skinny girl, wearing a dress her mother had made. She had no father and would have trouble finding a husband. She was distinctly unpretty, her hairstyle comically unbecoming, and her patent-leather shoes would have better suited a child. The generosity of the priest's blessing brought a rare smile to her face, and she wore it all the way home.

The teacher was doing his best too. He had borrowed nine horses and divided up his students into groups of three and sent us off to pass on the news where there were no phone lines. We were to ask everybody to spread the word. Since the incident with the hammock, I hadn't been out to the neighboring ranches, and I'd never done it on horseback. The journey was beautiful. Cranes soared up at our approach, flamingos were nesting in the lake beside our path, and the wide river, with its waters low, was thronged with lizards. The horses had problems in the slippery mud. Everywhere the vegetation threatened to swallow us and we suffered a multitude of bites from the insects we roused. We left messages in three locations. The people there agreed to pass the news on to others. The priest and the teacher invited one and all to come into Agustini on Sunday, for their friend had been murdered, a good man who had sought the welfare of all, justice, fair wages, better working conditions. And for that his enemies had killed him. That was the message we left, but who knows in what garbled form it was passed on. Whatever the form, the following Sunday found the town filled with more Indians than we had ever seen before.

37

Hospitality

The only hotel in Agustini was filled to bursting by Saturday night. Many households opened their doors, lending or renting out a room or a couple of beds or a hammock to the people who had traveled hour after hour to get there, some arriving the previous day, others unable to make it back home on the day of the funeral.

Amalia had taken in twenty visitors. She charged each one for the privilege of stretching out on lumpy mattresses or in decomposing hammocks, without even offering them a free glass of water, charging them cash for coffee, breakfast, bathroom privileges, and even the use of a towel.

But the patio of my own home played host to nobody. Grandma didn't even want to receive people we knew, like the friends of my mother's eternal suitor whom I'd bumped into as they searched for accommodations in the porticos and had brought back to the house. With a scowl harder than usual, and without my mother showing her face, she told them, "Sorry, gentlemen, but there's no place for you in this honest household."

That was it. Not one word more. She didn't even offer them a cooling drink, the minimum required by Agustini's laws of hospitality.

But all day long she went around talking to herself. She blamed everything on Old Baldy's stubbornness.

"I told him often enough, but, no, he wouldn't listen. Amalia told him as well. We both warned him in our own ways what he was up against. You don't fool around with people like them. Poor Irlanda [she was Old Baldy's wife], who's going to help her out now? Left alone with a boy to raise. What are they going to live on? They haven't a thing to call their own. He should have accepted one of those houses they kept offering him. That would have been enough to stop them from killing him, to stop them from stamping on him like a bug. I don't understand why some people have to make a problem out of everything. They just bring trouble on themselves and everybody else. How could they have killed him? It seems hardly two minutes ago I saw him going past the house chasing a hoop. He would be forever darting here and there, all over the town, running after that blessed hoop, I remember it perfectly, just like it was yesterday, just like it was this morning he went charging past. If he got a sniff of the coffee I was grinding, he put his hoop to one side, propped up against the fountain, and was into the kitchen to sit next to me till he got a taste of my soft, fresh chocolate. I remember him as a boy, just like it was yesterday. Why did he have to do this to us? Was it too much trouble to accept a little house, for the sake of all his loved ones, for the sake of us all who watched him grow up and thought so highly of him . . ."

38

The Seller of Scarves Returns

On the big day I got up at dawn, at the same time as Dulce and my grandmother.

"What on earth's gotten into you?" asked Dulce, staring at me in astonishment.

"I've got to be going. I'm off right now, can't stop. Just run the comb through my hair."

"What about breakfast?"

"No time for breakfast."

"You can cut out all the hurry," sounded my grandmother's voice from her room. "Nobody goes without breakfast in this honest household."

So I did have breakfast. After a chocolate drink and a fish-roe omelet I took off fast. The town was jammed with people. It was Sunday. The Indians were coming in for Mass, but they weren't disappearing into the aisles of the markets, they were crowding the streets. They strode along the sidewalks, staring straight ahead, and with them hundreds of people from all parts of the region and the whole length of the Gulf coast. From Tampico as far as Progreso people had come. Our isolated town had turned into a babel of voices. The streets were packed with people and cars.

of Oran, near the source of the Nile, and had enslaved its best stonemasons. The citizens of Oran were not warlike, so they had fortified their city with a patient cunning that kept it safe from assault. Our pirates had managed to capture it only by sinking to the basest of tricks. They got inside disguised as a troupe of northern comedians, singing Etruscan songs, dancing wildly, enchanting the women with their good looks, and bringing smiles to the faces of the kids. But once inside, they brandished their weapons and forced the people to name the best masons and describe what they looked like. Within no time they had rounded up the three smartest architects and twenty-five builders. These poor souls slaved away on the white cliffs of your father's island, constructing a famous defensive wall that nobody would even dream of attempting to assault. Its appearance was formidable. It gave an impression of being almost alive and that alone scared off would-be attackers. All they needed was one look at it to decide that the smart thing was to turn around and go back home. Those walls eliminated any need to ward off attacks. The three wise men of Oran also built a huge reservoir of water, so that the pirates didn't have to worry about being besieged, even for months on end. Inside the fortress lived the twelve founders. They alone knew all its secrets. Because once the building was finished, all the slave labor and the three architects had been put to the sword. They say that one after another these men were decapitated on the top of the walls so that their blood could stain it red and add to its sinister appearance. The stink of human blood was so rank that the birds and ducks that used to be the island's sole inhabitants no longer paused there on their annual migration south. The wise men must have realized that their dying blood would bring death to the pirates also. By scaring off the birds, the pirates had lost their natural food supply in case of a siege. Trapped inside their walls, they could not reach the fish in the sea. Maybe the three wise men of Oran were glad to die, happy to perish, since there was no practical possibility of rebuilding here the city at the source of the Nile. Maybe they knew of a door that opened on to Oran from the kingdom of the dead. Anything is possible.

"In the daily lives of the present inhabitants, people who are as gentle as they are indolent, nothing remains of that blood-thirsty character. They seem to have inherited the lifestyle of the people of Oran, perhaps because for generations they have lived in contact with the structures those people had built. There is only one vestige of the pirates still to be found. Each family, even though they are shepherds by trade, owns a small boat in which they honor a custom passed down from those piratical times. On summer nights, when the moon is full, they board their boats and make their leisurely way toward the horizon. Once they are on the open sea, they sing violent, discordant chanties, swaying crazily to the rhythms, the way their ancestors did prior to boarding a ship and plundering it. Then, all violence put aside, they head back to the coast, bathed in sweat from all that shouting and dancing, relieved to set foot again on the peaceful island.

"It's their custom to keep their boats tied up to the land, fastened to beams sunk into the sea especially for that purpose. They remain all year-round moored to the rocky cliffs, firmly anchored to the seafloor. They never pull them out of the water, like the people around here do, turning them upside down on the riverbanks to give them a chance to dry out once in a while. They're wet all the time, constantly in seawater. And there's a good reason for it. Nobody knows when this island, with its thirst for blood, with its grateful allegiance to the first inhab-itants who brought to its shores the best engineers of their day to fortify and beautify it—I mean, from time to time the island loses weight, and from time to time it demands its ration of blood. Once a year, as the dry summer is ending, the rough, reddish sand that lines all its beaches demands its tribute. The sand, looking more each day like dry, corrupted blood, calls out for its annual ration of new blood to maintain the weight of the island. The shepherds frantically sacrifice whole herds of adult and kid goats. They pretend it's a celebration, but really they're exorcising their fear. They dry the meat and then sell it in salty slices packed in baskets, offering it on the mainland as 'donkey meat'—it's got a good reputation for its exquisite taste—but first they let the blood run along narrow channels cut in the rocks and down to the sandy beaches and the sea. Once a year the island is surrounded by a ring of blood that takes months to finally dissolve.

"Till that happens, the island is in danger of losing weight. If there's some delay in slaughtering the animals, as well there can be because the inhabitants are such a laid-back lot, the island rises completely out of the sea. It would go drifting off through the air if it wasn't tethered by the boats. Their ropes stop it from floating away completely. But it hangs in the air there, trembling, till the shepherds sacrifice in tribute to their ancestors enough goats and lambs to satisfy its thirst and calm its itch to fly away."

The seller of scarves had ended his story, which he'd told without a pause, and he took a deep breath.

"I've told you where your father was born," he added. "You'll have to ask around to find out where he met your mother and how he fell in love with her. Ask Gustavo, if you like. I think you're old enough now to know the facts. You're a woman now, Delmira. The folks here are already picking out a husband for you, I bet. Get out in time. Go off with your father. I'll find him for you."

"You gave me a number to call. I still have it."

"Then it's up to you."

The words were barely out of his mouth before he began to pull down the tent, gathering in one scarf and shawl after another, till we found ourselves back in the noisy marketplace. He did not speak again, but he kept the smile on his face. I didn't speak, either.

Get out of here! The idea was delightful. Why not get out of here? I felt stained by the blood he had spoken of in his story. I was sure the hour for my departure had come. I would cross the ocean, seek the other side of my personal truth, nothing like the truth this salesman had tried to sell me. I didn't want adventures. I'd had enough of them already. I realized that the salesman had told me his story not because it was true but to offer me a connection, to build a bond between the two of us, because nobody in Agustini could tell you a story without plunging into fantasy. Maybe because of the climate or the proximity of the jungle or for reasons well beyond us, we all felt driven to tell ourselves tall tales. Personally, I yearned to see what the world was like where the world was logical, where nature obeyed the laws of physics without fail, where storytelling wasn't a universal habit but the prerogative of a few specialists with the designated task of studiously examining the nature of man and his world.

39

The Demonstration

I'd lost track of the time while I was listening to the seller of scarves. So I raced the rest of the way to the teacher's house. They were running off the last of the pamphlets that the teacher had written. Under my arm I was carrying a bunch of notes I'd scribbled down in the night.

"Excuse me, sir. I brought you these, excuse me—"

He ignored me.

"Can I make a stencil to print them off? I wrote all this."

"We haven't got time for anything now, Delmira."

"I can print them off myself, I promise."

"Go ahead," he said, mostly to shut me up.

They left me alone while I was still marking out the stencil and making rather a mess of it all. I printed off as many as I could, till I felt the need to go eat. By that time I had run off hundreds of copies of my pamphlet, to which I had appended my signature: Delmira of Agustini. This barely readable text was my first publication, and my only one before this present work. And I had committed the unforgivable error of inadvertently using the name of a great Uruguayan poet. An error which maybe ruined my career as a writer. Or maybe the reason was my foolish arrogance, a vanity that filled every corner of my soul. Or maybe it was my haste, my eagerness to see the world, to gobble down whole continents in a single mouthful, to suck up oceans and all their fish in one fell swoop. Or maybe it was the wild, revolutionary ideas I had absorbed at third hand while meditating on my actionless, endless, impractical novel, ideas that inspired me to write three dangerous paragraphs and thereby damage my literary future and in the process the whole of my life.

As soon as I was outside the door of the teacher's house, I began distributing my pamphlet to one and all. Some balladeers were singing a song they had improvised:

> *Old Baldy was a warrior.*
> *They went and shot him dead.*
> *But he is still among us,*
> *Though his body's full of lead.*

> *Though his body's full of lead, my friend,*
> *Baldy lives and always will.*
> *They can never kill Old Baldy*
> *For his spirit's with us still.*

> *His spirit's with us still, my friend*
> *For Baldy loved the poor.*
> *He's thinking of us all the time.*
> *Each day he loves us more.*

> *Each day he loves us more, my friend.*
> *So let us raise a cheer!*
> *We cannot lack for justice when*
> *Old Baldy's always here.*

I hung around with them, handing out my propaganda, sometimes listening to them, other times daring to join in. When they took a break, a young man came over to me. He was dressed in a white suit with brown shoes, with a straw hat, his outfit completely at odds with the clothes of the other demonstrators. Next to him came a photographer, and the two of them were visibly hot and tired.

"What's that you're handing out?"

"Something about the death of Old Baldy."

"Let me see." Then he added in a different tone, "My, but you're cute."

I smiled at him and handed him one of my pages. He took a second one from the pile, and the photographer snapped the musicians. Then they suddenly vanished. There were so many people around it was like looking for a needle in a haystack to find my classmates. By the time I found them, not a single one of my sheets was left.

The demonstration lasted all afternoon. We walked back to the street alongside the public gardens, men and women together, but our numbers were so great that we couldn't all get in. The end of the line, where we were, started to trample on those in front, until the teacher who was in control of us halted us completely. All the surrounding streets were jammed tight. We spilled over into the park itself, into the flowerbeds. From the bandstand, where the orchestra normally played its Sunday melodies, the teacher and a young fellow from the union harangued us. The crowd bellowed its approval, chanted slogans, and sang songs. A violent emotion swept us all off our feet, so different from the churchy feelings of Sunday Mass, when the priest addressed his passive, motionless congregation. What must he have been thinking as he saw this? What must he have felt as the tide of emotion surged through the breasts of his normally unresponsive parishioners, many of whom were in church only out of loyalty to him? What would he answer now when challenged to assess the faith of his flock? We had all heard him say, "In this town nobody believes in anything. If you're hungry, all you need do is raise a hand and grab a banana. If you're thirsty, you bend down to drink. If you want anything more elaborate, you stick your hand in the river and pull out a big fish. The heat of the day will cook it for you. All you have to do is pop it in your mouth. Who feels any fear of the Lord in those circumstances? These people here don't even believe there's a Creator, everything comes so easy to them, so ready to hand. They've got no worries. They've got no conscience to tell them right from wrong. On the slightest pretext they chop each other to pieces with machetes. Then they just as easily forget what the fight was all about, like nothing had happened. Life here is just a ghastly joke . . ."

40

A Scolding

That Sunday night I got back late to the house, so I had to bang on the door till they opened it. It was Grandma who let me in, her white hair loose about her shoulders, while Dulce looked on with alert eyes, waiting to see what Grandma would say to me. Before dropping the bar into place she spat out at me, "Disgusting troublemakers, that's what you all are!" She was furious. I went into my bedroom without closing the door behind me. Dulce didn't follow, either to do my hair or to offer me supper, staying beside my grandmother, sharing her rage, into which Grandma had no doubt indoctrinated her. I'd taken off only my sandals and was on the point of lowering my jeans when I heard Grandma's voice.

"Dulce, what are you thinking of? Go and see if the kid wants anything for supper and pick up her clothes so that she doesn't leave the place a mess. In the meantime, I'll secure the door and you can come back to do my hair. With all this coming and going it's gotten into a complete tangle. Maybe combing it out will calm me down. I'm all of a dither."

I was sitting on my bed, with my pants undone, when Dulce came into my room, prematurely aged, without a trace of youthfulness, eaten alive by the two bony creatures of the household, the smooth one and the round, her head covered by her rebozo, her feet shoeless as always. She looked me in the eyes and then immediately glanced away, but contact had been made. Our two bodies felt the presence of each other in the room. If she hadn't exchanged that glance with me, I'd have proceeded to take off my pants in front of her and toss them on the floor, and after them my panties, and hurl away my blouse with a careless fling of my arm over my head, and flip my earrings and necklace, maybe, onto the bed, while she picked up one garment after the other, saying nothing, folding up the clean ones, smoothing out the rumpled stuff, taking away the dirty clothes to wash, like a shadow, effective and unobserved. She'd also have put my tire-soled sandals onto the shoe rack, my earrings and necklace into the jewelry box. But since we'd exchanged glances, we both sat down. I wasn't going to strip naked now in front of this girl who'd grown old before her time, courting resentment and prematurely resigned to it, but she felt uncomfortable too, not knowing what to do in front of someone who normally didn't notice her presence, a woman of about her age but with a radically different lifestyle, whom she'd been used to waiting on since she was seven years old, working efficiently but without any personal contact, replacing it with abruptness and yells, like a machine whose functions had been determined by long tradition. I felt embarrassed in front of her, both by myself and by the role it had been my fate to adopt. Together, we two composed one personality, we were the two fragmented halves of one being. On her side, she shared a conspiratorial warmth with my grandmother, though it condemned her to servitude. On mine, I had a room of my own.

The slogans that we'd recently been shouting still rang in my ears. All day long I'd heard instant recipes for saving mankind and promises that the Revolution was coming, sailing this way across the Gulf of Mexico, in a boat headed from nearby Cuba, under a flag bearing the feather and sickle. I had handed

41

Grandmother's Story

"Today I'm going to tell you about the time the Indians got the *alushes* to start walking. You see, when I was a kid, about six or seven years old, it was still usual for Indians to have statues of *alushes* at the entrance to their houses. The *alushes* looked like tiny people, thin, with pronounced features, their arms crossed, wearing around their waist a sort of skirt made from corn leaves. The complete figure was no bigger than a just-ripened corncob. The little man or little woman emerged from the foliage in place of the cob itself, and their lines were so delicate it was hard to believe that the Indians could have made them with their own hands, since we're used to seeing them make such crude figures, with the look of monsters, when they don't look like cooking vessels nobody's had the goodness to give a finishing touch to. For sure, my nanny, Lupe, said that these clay figures actually grew out of the corn plant itself, that nobody but God could have made them with his hands, but how were we supposed to believe that God went around giving credence to the superstitions of Indians."

Grandma was looking for a chance to provoke me, because she realized I always bridled when she made disparaging remarks about Indians, and that I defended them with increasing vehe-

mence, obsessed by the issue, but on this occasion I made no
reply, for I wasn't going to take the bait and she wasn't going to
get a rise out of me. If she wanted, she could deny Indians had
souls and the power to reason, that was her business. My *tamal,*
an Indian concoction for sure, was delicious. My chocolate was
just right too, covered in froth, and I was worn out. Dulce had
already given Grandma's hair its first combing, and all the while
they'd probably chatted about what they'd heard tell of the demonstration—the gossip spreading among the rich folk of the town,
scared by the presence of so many people, all because of the death
of that troublemaker, Old Baldy, "nothing but out-and-out
commies who've come here to stir up the Indians"—and since
Dulce had made such a smooth job of it, she was already plaiting
the hair, before the nightly story had barely gotten under way.

"The Indians, I was telling you, had one or more *alushes* in
front of their houses. There were those who placed them by the
door hinges, others nailed them to one side or other of the
doorframe, while some stuck them in the ground at both sides.
At one Indian house that I went into with my papa—it was a
scorching-hot noonday, and we were on horseback, with his
men, checking out something or other on the farm—they gave
us some coffee to drink in these enormous mugs, scalding-hot
coffee, brewed in a clay pot with sugar and cinnamon, so that
we could 'cool off,' they said. I'd have given a king's ransom for
a glass of chilled soda pop. But back then, in those heat waves,
in the middle of the jungle, without ice or fridges, well—in fact,
I think they still don't have electricity out there even now, no
doubt because the Indians said no when the government offered
it to them, because there's nobody more stupid than those people,
total sticks-in-the-mud when it comes to changing their beliefs,
so used to living in misery that they even enjoy it, and if I'm
wrong about that, then explain to me why they choose to live

in such appallingly hot places where you can't even build a decent road, because . . ."

Dulce had finished dressing Grandma's hair and had now started combing out mine, while I was eating the last of my *tamal,* which was quite glorious. Without taking her eyes off Dulce, Grandma turned to face me.

"Then the *alushes* started to stir and move. It was when this region had its worst drought ever, much longer than the one we suffered through a couple of years back, and the coffee beans withered and not even a blade of new grass was to be seen, and only the trees managed to survive, though they produced no fruit, not one mamey or banana or mango or papaya, absolutely nothing. Anyway, one day all the *alushes* left the doorways of the Indian shacks, and turned into creatures of flesh and blood, talking among themselves in their own language, and there wasn't a single spot anywhere where you didn't hear their strange mutterings and there wasn't a single house where they didn't get up to their tricks. An *alushe* would show up here and there, making a horse skid in its tracks, tossing a little girl out of her swing, throwing a seesaw out of balance, removing the plug from the fountain, putting too much salt in the food, knocking over cooking pots, and pulling off the tablecloths after the table had been set. Every day that went by, they got bolder and bolder, and if you heard their mutterings here and there at first, it wasn't long before you heard their cackling laughter. Soon their shouts became an everyday thing in the center of town. We learned to keep our mouths shut, because if we told a secret to somebody, some *alushe* or other would soon be shouting it out till the whole of Agustini knew. If we did anything really private and personal, we ran the risk of the *alushes* broadcasting it far and wide. They gave my grandfather diarrhea and went around chanting, 'Old Melo's got flu in his asshole.' They started to grow bigger, and went from causing us major and minor irritations and lots of embarrassment to breaking the law. They stole corn, they stole coffee, they stole pumpkin seeds, they stole cocoa and sugar, and bags of flour, and sacks of rice from the market. It was uncanny how tiny creatures could carry off such heavy loads to the Indians. And one day, because of their pranks, we woke up without a thing to eat. Every cupboard was bare; there wasn't one they spared, while the crafty Indians went around wearing faces like nothing had happened, just their faces of course, because their bellies were stuffed with our chocolates and our cheeses, our hams and our flour. Somebody had a dream that showed him that these uncivilized critters, who knew only how to handle maize, would meet in the evenings to eat the pick of our wheat by the handful, dying of laughter at us because of our habit of eating this stuff, not realizing, of course, that we ground the wheat and baked it in the oven to make it into bread, and he also dreamed that when they were covered from head to toe in flour, they decided to toss the rest of it into the river. I've no doubt his dream was true, because I never saw them giving us back anything that the *alushes* had stolen from us. And we still didn't get a drop of rain, thanks to those *alushes*.

"Then the *alushes* started to take our possessions, first things that didn't matter, costume jewelry, then really valuable things, coins of precious metal that we kept hidden in trunks, necklaces from our grandmothers, gold chains with a thousand gems in them, and it was then, and not until then, that we decided to put a stop to these tiny creatures. But how could we do it, when we couldn't catch an *alushe*? You'd see one here, and the next minute he'd be on the other side of town. So we had to organize a clean sweep of the *alushes*. Early one Sunday, just as dawn was breaking, the men from the town got together in the town center, carrying all their weapons. Without a word said, they marched to the highway and halted on the outskirts of Agustini.

At any Indian they saw coming that way, they opened fire. They killed a few dozen, till one of them managed to escape the hail of bullets and told the others and no more came. The corpses stayed in a pile all day, like a fence that forced the *alushes* to return to their clay shapes and quit their pranks. Maybe hundreds died. I was only six, so my mother didn't let me see the corpses, but in the night I heard the Indians coming to collect them, a multitude of Indians, looking for relatives, mourning them, weeping out their dirges. They loaded them up and took them away, and by the following morning there wasn't a single corpse left, and all talk of naughty, thieving *alushes* was a thing of the past.

"That's the way stories end in Agustini, Delmira. Here people kill. You haven't seen anything yet, but here, when they feel threatened, the owners of the farms kill. And they're right to do so, because there's no other way to keep order. So be careful, girl. I'm telling you this without anger, without raising my voice, only because I want you to know. If you don't care about yourself, at least remember that we have two women in this house who have always lived innocent lives and who never deserved . . ."

Her lecture went on for a few more minutes, till she stretched out her shawl and curled up under it. Dulce lay down at her feet, the shawl was tucked in tighter, and the pair of them fell into a deep sleep, while I stayed awake, thinking about the *alushes*. I thought I heard a noise in Mama's room, as if she was moving the water jug around, but that was the last thing I was aware of. I too was exhausted. It had been far too long a Sunday.

42

A Little Girl
Gets Carried Off

I didn't have a single dream in the course of that long night, and I didn't regain consciousness till I was awakened by screams and yells that seemed to come from the street. I stretched my limbs as lazily as I could. My grandmother had closed my door so that I could sleep in, as usual, in the mornings, and so I washed at my leisure and put on my underwear. My only pair of jeans was outrageously dirty, so I got my miniskirt out of the wardrobe, along with a matching blouse and a pair of stockings. I got dressed, slipped on some shoes, and opened the door to tell Dulce to come and comb my hair.

Then I was overcome by a longing for my grandmother to come and entertain me with one of her stories, something to occupy my attention. I was thinking about that, absurdly, and talking to myself. "Tell me a story, Grandma, tell me a story."

"What's the kid saying?" Ofelia asked Dulce. When she saw my door open, Dulce had hurried to join me, as if combing my hair would bring her the serenity our house badly needed, and Ofelia had tagged along, horrified.

"Don't pay her any attention. She's been known to go a bit batty on us," Dulce answered, pulling on my arm to get me to react and dragging me along to the kitchen.

In the patio of the house corpses were assembled, some in heaps, others in rows. A squad of men had brought them there, some of the bodies still warm. When they brought in the first ones, they'd hammered on the door, although it was open, to summon Grandma. A dark-complexioned man, standing to attention, had said to her in the accents of Vera Cruz, "Orders, ma'am. And orders are orders."

After him the other soldiers filed in, laying one body beside another, till they ran out of space, and then they piled them one on top of another.

The clatter of their boots had not wakened me, or even filtered into my dreams. I'd simply heard nothing. Grandma closed the door and called Mama. They dressed hurriedly and went looking for the priest to find out what was behind it all.

It was when they came back with him and some of the relatives of the victims that I awoke. These poor souls ran here and there around the patio, identifying the dead and pulling them out of the piles and stacking back up those they didn't know, people who had come from as far afield as Tampico and Ciudad del Carmen to bury Old Baldy. The relatives grieved over the dead and the priest gave them his blessings, but he couldn't say anything more because he was in total shock.

Many of the corpses were practically mincemeat. The lucky ones had received only a few bullets, but the others had been beaten to death and everybody without exception had gotten a bullet in the back of the head.

Dulce sent Ofelia to bring the hairbrush to do my hair, while she tried to get me to swallow my hot chocolate and the carrot juice she had prepared. Then the soldiers came back into the patio.

They asked to speak with my grandmother, explaining that they'd come to take what belonged to them.

"You mean the dead? Get rid of those in the basin of the fountain. Their families have already come to claim the others."

"No, ma'am, the dead are staying here, they're your problem, we've finished with them. We came for Delmira, the one from Agustini."

"The little girl?"

"We came to pick up Miss Delmira, the agitator from Agustini."

"Listen to me, Officer, the whole town went into the streets with the rebels yesterday. Don't take our little girl."

Their only response was to put in her hands the newspaper from Villahermosa. Then they repeated the phrase that they'd rattled off when they brought in the bodies. "Orders, ma'am. And orders are orders."

"They're looking for the kid," Ofelia told us, her eyes staring, as she came into the kitchen.

"Who's looking for her?"

"The soldiers. They're going to take her away."

I felt that I'd peed myself, although, in fact, I hadn't. I was suddenly plunged deep inside myself in a way I'd never felt before. It came close to the feeling I'd had in the bakery, but there was something extra to it that overwhelmed the similarity. Was it terror or panic? But I didn't cry or breathe a word. I didn't move, either. The soldiers came for me in the kitchen. They lifted me out of the chair. I grabbed the handle of the meat grinder with one hand—that was my only form of resistance—and it came away from the grinder. I was carried, feet off the ground, out of the kitchen, still clutching the handle. We crossed the patio, the passageway, the heavy door. Mama and Grandma were waiting for me on the sidewalk.

"If you're taking her away, you can take me as well," said Grandma.

"No, not you, Mother," shrieked Mama, grabbing on to her skirt, like a child. "Not you!" Her eyes were tearless, but she never once gave me so much as a glance.

The soldiers dropped me on the ground. Then I realized I was carrying the handle of the meat grinder, and without a word I handed it to my grandmother, saying, "Here you are. Look after it."

"Delmira, that business with the *alushes*. I shouldn't have mentioned it. I brought you bad luck. I summoned them and brought demons into the house."

There must have been between twelve and fifteen soldiers surrounding us. The two who had hauled me out of the kitchen handed me over to the rest of the squad. They came up and tied my arms together with unnecessary force, then one of them yanked up my hands to put handcuffs on my wrists. My hands were in front of me, loaded with chains, as if I were the first white slave in Agustini. The soldiers opened up a gap in their ranks, exposing my slavelike condition, and once again I saw Mama, Grandma, Dulce, Ofelia, along with Lucifer, Petra, and the kitchen helpers. Little Delmira was a slave of the cropped-headed military, dark-skinned men from far away, who, if they'd come from Agustini, wouldn't have dared raise a finger against the daughter and grand-daughter of the Ulloa family, the founders of Agustini, where streets were named for them, where benches in the park and the church and the cemetery carried their august name. For hundreds of years the Ulloas had been masters of Agustini.

A pair of soldiers grabbed their prisoner and with a few pushes showed her the way to go. No white-skinned person had ever walked the streets of Agustini in this fashion, never had been paraded like this, with wrists bound by metal, tied up like a dog, as docile as any dog, because I put up no resistance, striding along where their jabs and pushes told me to go. We turned the corner. I looked back, but my house was no longer in sight. Nobody had followed me. However, a few paces behind, a mule trotted after us. The soldier boys started to threaten me. "Let's see if this knocks some sense into the little bitch. Hey, blondie, you don't have a clue what's in store for you, do you? This little bird is gonna sing, and how."

From every balcony of the town they saw me go by. On every street they stood on the sidewalk watching me pass, because the soldiers chose to lead me down the middle of the road, the place for dumb animals, donkeys, horses, and cars. Blond Delmira had lost her status in Agustini, at the hands of those creeps who kept dragging her along without pity, for no good reason. Agustini was not raising its voice in my defense. It didn't seem to be the same town as the day before, where one and all, in total solidarity, had welcomed the protest against the murder of Old Baldy. This was a town in terror, a town that didn't understand what was going on, a town under the control of a power wholly foreign to it. But neither did any witch fly over me or toads leap out into our path. No albino crocodile used its tail to block the passage of the two pigs who were manhandling me more and more offensively. The pictures of the saints didn't dance, but everything in the town struck a pose and then came tumbling down, though the birds did keep on flying. The leaves on the cocoa pods and coffee plants had their tips all shriveled, but their fruits, almost ready to be picked, remained unharmed. The pitayas didn't rot, the mangoes didn't rot, the papayas didn't fall, and the bananas showed no reaction to the first white slave in Agustini, only the leaves of the plants, as if an unexpected frost had arrived that morning, a frost that the plants themselves could take lightly, without too much concern.

Dr. Camargo came out of his house when he saw me go by. He, apparently, was not aware of anything that had happened that morning in Agustini, nobody could have gone to tell him or ask for his assistance, by a stroke of good luck leaving him without a single wound to heal. He came out dressed in his pajamas, with a dressing gown on top. Clad like that, he was the only resident of Agustini who came to my defense. Stopping in front of my two custodians, he stared at me with a look of compassionate surprise, and said to them, "Gentlemen, whether or not you have to take her away, I'll stand surety for her before the law. I'm the doctor of this town, Dr. Camargo, at your service, and I've no cause to stick my nose in here. But you ought to know—though apparently you don't, because you're not from around here—that we don't treat young ladies this way."

With two blows to his face they laid him on the ground, making him bleed, one of his eyebrows pouring out blood. The mule still trotted after us, as if we were some kind of fascinating carrot, and almost collided with him, except that Sara and Dorita, his wife and daughter, ran and picked him up, scaring the stupid animal which seemed more like a hyena than a mule because it showed no sign of letting the carrion out of its sight. Nobody else in the neighborhood came to the doctor's rescue. What happened to you that morning, Agustini? Did the blood of strangers and of your own kin darken the light of reason? Did your magic that day consist of tying down your people with inescapable fear?

The majority of the demonstrators had already left Agustini. The soldiers had massacred those heading toward the market in the light of dawn. The Indians who had come down from the hills to sell seeds or bundles of fruit also formed part of the slaughter. Most of the others, when they learned of the crime, had run off to warn Villahermosa, Tampico, and Mexico City. Others had caught the eight o'clock bus, fleeing from the horror and trying to forget it. Two buses belonging to the union had left, completely packed with its members.

In the central park, groups of visitors clustered around the bandstand, standing shoulder to shoulder and back to back, without daring to look one another in the eye and barely uttering a word. The soldiers, I don't know if out of a wish to provoke them, crossed the park with me in front of them, passing to one side of them. They all turned toward me. I recognized some faces I had gotten to know the day before. One of them belonged to the man I'd found a hammock for at the Juarezes' place, and over there stood another who'd arrived with his doctor's briefcase to see what was going on, and over there the reporter in the light suit who'd asked me for a copy of my pamphlet and called me cute.

"Can we take your photos?" he asked the soldiers. "Just to show how well you're doing your duty. I'm from the *Tabasco Sun,* the government daily."

We halted in front of him, with the stupid mule still following us.

"Well, of course."

The photographer, who had snapped the musicians the previous day, was eating an ice cream at one of the tables of the ice-cream parlor. His companion called him over. "Hey, look what a great photo I got you!" He came running toward us. For the first photo the soldiers did nothing special. The two who had their hands on my buttocks and back moved them to my shoulders, clasping them like two hooks.

For the second they lifted up my skirt.

For the third one of them hugged me shamelessly.

For the fourth they made me kneel down and lay my face on the ground while one of them put his enormous boot on my back.

The reporter didn't dare ask them for a fifth, seeing that with each photo they were turning into bigger and bigger bullies.

"Thanks, you guys. Why have you taken her prisoner?"

"For revolutionary activities. We've just left the evidence with her grandmother. This is Delmira, the girl from Agustini."

The reporter was startled. He didn't know I was Delmira, but what he did know was that he was the one who had told them about me. He didn't work for the government daily, which belonged to the governor's brother. He reported, in fact, for the *Villahermosa Daily*. He was the one who, the day before, had called the paper to tell them word for word what the flyers we were giving out said, so that they could publish it on the first page. It was because of that article that they were now taking me away as their prisoner, the article he'd had published, and with it he'd condemned me to prison.

"Is she the one who published that thing in the *Villahermosa Daily*?"

"Dead right she is. Now she's going to find out what happens to blondes who act like little bitches. We're gonna clean up this town before the day's out."

"Can I ask the girl a question, guys?"

"Go ahead."

"In the meantime, my friend, the photographer, invites you all to an ice cream."

The soldiers gave a pleased laugh and clustered around the counter of the ice-cream parlor.

"Do you want me to tell anybody, Delmira? I'm really sorry. I'm to blame for this mess. I don't know what else I can do to help you."

He explained to me rapidly who he was. I gave him the phone number of my uncle Gustavo. "He's my mother's brother, Gustavo Ulloa, the engineer." He was startled again to hear my surname. "Yes, don't jump out of your skin. We're the Ulloas of Agustini. I'm sure he can get me away from these cavemen. He'll have a word with the governor. They're friends." And at the same time I gave him my father's number and my paternal family name, explaining, "He's Italian. He lives in London. Tell him to get me out of here." The reporter took rapid notes, then,

43

The Telephone Operator

To make long-distance calls, remember, you had to go through the telephone office. You couldn't just dial the number from home. You dialed zero and then asked to be connected to your long-distance number. The reporter dialed zero from the grocery store, which had just opened, his feet in puddles of water as they were washing the floor. He got no answer. He dialed zero again.

"They aren't answering?" asked the girl who was scrubbing the floor. "Hadn't you better go over to the office? Teresita's a daydreamer. She takes ages to answer. It's just around the corner. Out here."

The girl accompanied the man into the street and pointed out the way he should go. "Keep going to the corner and turn up there, and *bingo!* there you are!" And she pointed her arm once again to show him where.

He'd hardly turned the corner when he saw the metal sign sticking out of the wall, with a telephone painted on it, indicating where to go. The door of the office was ajar. Nobody was sitting in front of the telephone board. All there was was a folded piece of paper. The calendar was opened to the current date. The operator was hanging from the fan, hanged by a telephone cord. The inert body of Teresita was the only thing that day in Agustini not touching the ground, defying the law of gravity, disrupting the natural order of the world. Beneath her shoeless feet, which were still rocking back and forth, lay a chair kicked aside, the one in which she had spent so many hours embroidering, knitting, dreaming, connecting calls, and which minutes before had been her means to death. On the telephone, a folded sheet of paper carried the message: "Please give to Father Lima." The reporter opened it. In pencil, in a shaky, childlike hand, she had written the following:

Dear Father,

The three soldiers who came looking for me at home raped me, saying it was because I helped the rebels bring people to the town. They raped me in front of my blind mother. I kept my mouth shut and didn't say anything when I went out. I didn't want her to know about it, poor thing. Please, go visit her and comfort her. I'm leaving her alone. It breaks my heart but I can't go on living with this. Please give me forgiveness, don't let me suffer among the sinners, give me absolution. God knows I can't do anything else. Forgive me, I beg you, make sure that my soul finds peace. Say a Mass for me.

Teresita

The reporter went to the door and called for help. Nobody appeared. He knocked on the open door of the house that abutted on the office and explained to Señora Lupe what had happened.

"The Lord save her. She was the finest being who ever lived in this town, an innocent angel. How could they have done this?"

"I need to make a phone call. Can anyone help me?"

Señora Lupe's daughter helped him make the long-distance connection. First of all he called my uncle Gustavo in Mexico City. He explained the situation while Gustavo remained silent, not saying a word. The call had awakened him and he took a few moments to react. The reporter asked Gustavo to tell Delmira's father and gave him his phone number.

"Where did Delmira get his number?" was what Gustavo wanted to know.

"Do it for her sake, right now. The soldiers who showed up this morning have killed loads of people. They raped the telephone operator. I have her here in front of me."

"Teresita?"

"Yes, that's who I think it is. If you know anybody, do something immediately. These guys aren't fooling around. It's dead serious."

"I'm on my way right now. And tell Teresita that those bastards—"

"Teresita has killed herself, sir."

"Teresita?"

"The soldiers raped her. They accused her of helping to organize what went on yesterday, and she killed herself."

"You don't mean she's right there in front of you?"

"She's right here, sir. Hanging by a cable in front of my eyes. We're still waiting for the boys to come get her down."

Gustavo was stunned. He couldn't stay in bed having heard what he'd heard. As soon as he hung up, he leapt out of bed. Meanwhile, the reporter was on the phone to the *Villahermosa Daily,* but they told him they weren't sure they could publish that kind of stuff. He hung up and called the *Excelsior* in Mexico City and told them everything that had happened.

"There's enough for us to put an item in the Stop Press section. Will you call us back at midnight and give us your copy, for tomorrow's edition? What's your number?"

"The girl at the telephone office killed herself. The soldiers raped her," the reporter said again. "She's right here in front of me. Her feet have stopped swinging now. I don't know if your calls will get through. I'll be in the Ulloa Hotel. If you haven't phoned by twelve-thirty, I'll come back to the office and try to call you."

44

Prison and Flight

Up to that time the police department in Agustini had been a laughingstock. Lucho Aguilar, the tenant of Amalia, Old Baldy's aunt, was the younger brother of the mayor of Ciudad del Carmen. Thanks to family influences, he had gotten a government position and had ended up there, as did everybody else who had no skill at anything in particular. The police in Agustini collected the drunks off the street and carted them to the jail to sleep off the booze—and that was the limit of their effectiveness. Otherwise people dealt out their own justice. There was one policeman in the town, plus his boss. The policeman strolled about the town at nightfall, sporting a whistle, announcing that all was well, while his boss picked his nose in public and in private gorged on oranges from Amalia's patio, parroting at this or that party some idea or other he'd borrowed from his brothers. I already mentioned that when he smiled he had the look of an imbecile or of genius endowed with a disconcerting cunning. Maybe he was a bit of both, because now that the only room in the jail was packed with people of different ages and social classes, he knew at once what to do. He remembered the henhouses that everybody else had forgotten, another of my uncle Gustavo's youthful enterprises, which finally neither earned him a penny nor lost him one, because two strokes of good luck let him dispose advantageously of the unsalable hens. He set up a darts stall—hit ten bull's-eyes in a row and you went home with a roasted chicken—where there was a lineup for weeks of people wanting to try their skill, and he sold feather pillows, which rotted away before the summer was out, either because the climate wreaked havoc with them or because the feathers weren't properly treated, though who could say, since they were the first and last feather pillows ever sold in Agustini.

Anyway, the police chief took the special prisoners to the henhouses, the schoolteacher, the priest, and the one and only Delmira, along with the most repulsive bunch of soldiers he could find, his unfailing animal instinct having selected the most cocky, violent, and bestial ones around. We were locked in pens where the hens once lived, in separate rooms, for I don't know how many hours, plus the minutes my uncle Gustavo spent waiting for the governor to show up at his office because he wasn't at home or with his mistress, a woman famous all over Tabasco—maybe he was with his boyfriend, but nobody had his phone number to check—plus the time it took to explain things to the governor who didn't have a clue what they were talking about, plus the time it took the governor to get in touch with Agustini, now that nobody was manning the telephone booth. One of his secretaries had the bright idea to send a telegram, saying: "Delmira is a member of my family," signed by the governor, and that was enough to stop the beastly soldiers from scrabbling under my skirts and hunting down the juiciest parts of my body.

The telegraph operator in Agustini, a kindly soul who was a friend of the priest, added the words which saved two lives: "and go easy on the priest and the teacher."

In spite of the telegram they didn't set us free. They put all three of us together in a single room, while they went to check if the message really had come from the governor. They spoke by phone to the main barracks; the people there made contact with the governor's personal secretary and he told them that it was true, that the governor had tried to speak personally with the people in Agustini, but realizing he couldn't get through, he'd sent the telegram.

"And so why didn't he contact the main barracks?" they asked.

The secretary didn't give them an answer. Instead, he thought, "What a cuckoo I am! In all the panic and haste it never occurred to me to do the sensible thing."

They freed us at sunset. Uncle Gustavo, who was in town by this time, was waiting for us at the police department. He put me in his car and drove me out of town. I never saw the house of my grandmother again. I never saw her again. I never saw my mother again. She died six years later. I didn't go to the funeral, although Gustavo insisted I should. In a letter Grandma explained at length how it was that Mama had fallen sick, with a black patch first appearing on her back at one side of her left shoulder blade, as if somebody had given her a hard punch. But it didn't hurt or sting, and the doctor said not to worry about it. Then she started to have problems in her left arm, in the area of her armpit. Here an ulcer broke out and it started to get bigger and bigger. It became infected and however many sulfa powders from the doctor she sprinkled on it, and for all the honey and compresses from the herbalist she spread on it, it still continued to grow. Then a wart began to grow right in the center of the black patch on her back, which she still had not been able to get rid of. She lost her appetite and said she felt tired all day long. She said she woke up tired, that she had problems sleeping. She had given up the hammock and now slept on a bed of sugar that Grandma had had built. Instead of a mattress it had several kilos of sugar and was surrounded by a little channel of water to keep the ants away.

She slept there because she said that only the sugar gave her any relief from her open wounds.

One morning they found her dead. "Her agonies are over" were Grandma's words. "I still don't have white hair, but she's already gone and died on us. The doctor said it was a massive heart attack. As if her skin condition wasn't enough to finish her off! Well, in my opinion, she did die of a heart problem, but not in the sense he meant. She rotted from the inside out. That was the rottenness that killed her." I believed my grandmother's explanation, perhaps for the first time in my life. Mama was still young, but she hadn't found herself another boyfriend or an official suitor since she'd separated from my father. Father Lima hadn't lived in Agustini for the past five years or so. He'd asked that they send him to Tehuantepec, where, according to the gossip my grandmother passed on, he had an Indian woman who "was driving him out of his mind with desire." Mama could have gotten involved with any other man in town, but she got in over her head with him and there she drowned, longing for her absent love.

My grandmother's long letters replace her nightly tales, but they lack the old burning imagination. She's agreed to give me exhaustive accounts of what goes on in Agustini. So I know that the great-grandson of Doña Luz who used to stink of urine hasn't gotten married, that Dulce still works in the house, that Lucifer still carries on as cook, that the aunt of the schoolteacher fell sick but got better, that the schoolmaster took off, some saying he went to live with the Indians in the jungle, others that he was murdered, and still others that he goes around armed, causing problems for the government. The chief of police, Lucho Aguilar, was assassinated one day in the covered walkway beside the square, nobody knows by whom, though after my disappearance there's a long list of why's. The worst thing that's happened in Agustini I don't need to tell you: They've destroyed the jungle.

Between the petroleum, the exploitation of the tropical forests, and the introduction of cattle, they've swept it all away. That marvel of nature was converted mainly into telephone poles and railway sleepers. There are no more mahogany trees, no red cedars, no chicozapotes. There are still mangrove swamps and popals and tulars, but only because these trees grow in water.

I passed through Mexico City, barely seeing a thing. I know nothing of it. I never laid eyes on the frescoes of Diego Rivera in the National Palace or the Cathedral or the University Stadium, or the Latin American Tower, or the building of the National Lottery, or the statues of Diana and the Angel of Independence. I never drove along the Avenida Reforma and I'm not sure if we even traveled a few blocks of Avenida Insurgentes, the longest avenue in the world, while we were heading straight to the airport. I never got to see the Zocalo in the heart of Mexico City or the Museum of Anthropology and History or the gigantic statues of Tlaloc or Coatlicue or Coyolxauhqui. I didn't even sleep in the city.

My uncle Gustavo's secretary was waiting for us at the British Airways counter with a passport he'd gotten for me through the help of an influential friend. I had a seven-hour flight to New York, but on this occasion I didn't get to know that place, either. I've gone back there since, but never back to Mexico City. I blew through Mexico City like a stray breeze and hardly had time to realize I was there. So there's no point in talking to me about "Mexico, beautiful and beloved" and other such tags from songs. I do know the curtain that hangs on the stage of the Palace of Fine Arts because I've seen it in some book or other. But the volcanoes can't stir me the way they do other Mexicans, nor can the view of the Valley of Mexico, because I never saw either Popo or Itza. I get nothing out of the nopal cactus or the maguey plant or the Indian with his serape whom I've seen in sketches here and there. I never visited Xochimilco or climbed the Pyramids

of the Sun and of the Moon at Teotihuacán. I never caught sight
of mariachis, but I suspect they sound different from the ones
they sometimes have here in Germany. I never saw *charro* horse-
men. In my town nobody celebrated the Day of the Dead. I never
knew the great mountain ranges of Mexico, nor its deserts, nor
its other cities. I tried tequila maybe a couple of years ago. I know
something about the rest of Tabasco only because I've read about
it, but I've no idea what the magisterial sky over Zacatecas looks
like or the Hill of the Chair overlooking Monterrey. I never
visited the Cabañas Hospice in Guadalajara with those glorious
frescoes by Orozco. I never went back to Mexico. Thirty years,
Delmira, thirty years. And before them, Agustini, with your eyes
fixed on a place that turns its back on the rest of the country.

1997

45

Thirty Years

I will finish my story in the style that Lope de Vega used in the novels dedicated to Marcia Leonarda. So here you won't get a blow-by-blow account of everything that happened; all I'm going to give you is a rapid sketch of the key events.

Ten years ago I was working on Lope de Vega, editing him in Spanish for German students taking Spanish courses, and I'm going to use that as my pretext for choosing this break-neck narrative style, instead of showing my readers the incidents as they happened. I'm going to follow the example of Lope, who polished off the end of his *Diana* in a mere ten lines. I can't dawdle over the thirty years I spent in Europe, because there was nothing in those thirty years to make me pause. I was alien to them, a complete Other. For three decades I didn't sleep in a hammock, I saw no strange objects floating in water. No albino crocodile popped into my room, no army of Indians came by sucking voluptuously on juicy insects, no legion of toads exploded against my balcony, there were no imposing witches hawking fake merchandise, no rainstorms purchased for cash. I've spent six times five years here without hearing once the nightly tale of my grandmother. I came here in search of a world that obeyed the laws of physics; it is now all around me, but I

can't say I've come to terms with it. The first years here I was
fascinated by the down-to-earthness of Europe, while the Europeans of my generation, I saw, were in turn being massively
seduced by our apparent lack of logic. I found my father and
then I lost him. Inspired by Lope, I forged various personalities, I believed myself first this person, then that, I showed distinct preferences for things and then I went and changed them,
I opted for pronounced tastes and styles and then I dropped
them. Once or twice I fell in love. I pretended I was working-
class, I passed as an aristocrat, people thought I was the daughter of a king, I wore gauze and tulle at the same time as I dyed
my hair and curled it coquettishly. I dressed like a man out of
love for a woman. I found my father again, only to lose him
again. I ended up beating him at his own game. These days
they've opened The Globe, Shakespeare's old theater, and I
ought to take advantage of the chance to go visit it, to see a
show there with him. We'll make a date to drink a pint or two
in his favorite pub. Maybe I'll get there fifteen minutes late
because of a delay on the Tube, while they check out if the
bomb scare is genuine, but he won't be aware of that. He'll
just sit there watching the froth move down his glass. The
minute he sets eyes on me, we'll launch into our chatter, as if
we'd seen each other only yesterday. I'll listen to his latest
calamity in love and we'll go off together in silence to sniff out
the bookstores in Charing Cross Road. Without realizing it,
we'll approach the banks of the Thames, arm in arm, and we'll
look at the originals of scenes we've so often seen reproduced
in photos. We'll sit down where the nobility once sat, like them
and now like everybody, with the rain on our backs. After the
show, we'll go dine where we have a view of the Thames, from
one of the new restaurants that they've built some way from
the City, where in times past stood a factory which had employed

child labor, which was then replaced by a warehouse, and which is now the last word in chic.

This is all I can tell you now, because my story starts and ends in Agustini. When I began this book, I'd planned to write only three brief pages about my town, and after that I'd describe the plane I took to escape from it, my journey beside a lady who took compassion on me for the story I told her and who left me in New York, where she offered me the book she'd been reading:

"*One Hundred Years of Solitude*—it's fantastic, you gotta read it, Del, everybody's reading it!"

Imagine my disappointment on flipping through its pages, telling myself that I didn't leave Agustini just to find other towns that resembled it. Then would come my arrival in London, the awful malaise of jet lag that nobody had warned me about, my meeting with my father, the experience of '68 at his side, my trip to Berlin, my job as an editor. Here I'd pause in my narrative to tell you about my sin, the one that ruined my life in Germany. Then, in the final chapter, I'd return to Agustini, only to find that it no longer existed—and that's all I'd have breath for. Those are really the pages I intended to write. That way Delmira Ulloa would have freed herself from her idiotic errors, signing her work with the name of a prodigious and inimitable writer, before dying maybe in a fit of passion. My book would have freed me from the tangle of events that had surrounded me. After all, I fled here to write. But it didn't turn out that way. I avoided my encounter with the truth to meet up once again with my past, my infancy. That, after all, was my real life, the only one I could ever truly be faithful to.

Time has moved on while I've been telling the story of my town. A chilly spring with its fragile miracle has come and gone. Summer arrived, a spurious summer with gusts of wind and rain. The sun had hardly decided to take up residence in the sky and it was August already! Suddenly Berlin has burst out into greenery and light. People are coming back from their summer vacations with their skin brown, faces aglow, throbbing with energy. The city is full of visitors from other parts of Germany, some with kids, some without. Holiday times are staggered here so that the favorite places to relax don't get swamped with millions of visitors.

But I've prolonged the winter in my apartment. I go out little. I work at home, I write at home. It looks as if I've left my life in the lurch in order to prolong it, like some paradoxical form of gymnastics. Today I crossed the Tiergarten in all its renewed greenery—it's the central park where I walk and intended to replace the bandstand in Agustini, though that was never my conscious decision. Couples were lying naked on the grass, exchanging caresses; on the beach men were wooing other men without a stitch on; mothers were getting grouchy with their kids, and from his van the ice-cream seller was dispensing his ephemeral merchandise, stuff the heat makes popular but which the sun melts into trickles.

Life continues on. But not for me. Here ends the life I lived as a girl, the way the other lives I've invented have ended. Now it's my turn to invent myself over again. But concluding this account of my doings has left me exhausted. So I'll take off to the beach, to Cumaná or Costa Rica, or to Djerba or New Zealand. I'll try not to think about anything while I sunbathe, pretending I'm German. Then I'll invent another character for myself and, if I'm lucky, I'll decide to be a writer, with stories to tell on the written page, but stories unlike this one, stories that aren't autobiographical and actually happened, but stories where the fantasy makes a certain kind of sense, where metaphor and meaning underwrite each other's mechanisms, and where imagination

come back from the beach, or if I'll have the nerve to return to
Agustini and look again at the house where I was a girl, my grandmother now an old crone for sure, my uncle the governor, the
nuns all wrinkled, Young Baldy the rector of the University of
Villahermosa, Dulce probably as ageless as ever, Lucifer raving
mad, Dr. Camargo without a scrap of hair, the streets choked
with vehicles, Agustini grown out of shape, the home of a hundred times more inhabitants, the apartment blocks built by
Gustavo lining the whole coastline. I don't know if I dare climb
the church belfry and view the endless expanse of ranches, the
paved highways, the mobs of people coming in and out of the
market which my uncle also built. Worse still, I don't know if,
while evening shadows fall, I'll have the courage to see, from
up there, the frozen light of the TV screens flickering out from
every window, instead of young and old strolling through the
streets, eating corn on the cob, circling and circling the bandstand, looking for the young woman who makes those exquisite
chunky tortillas from fresh dough, crammed with pork sausage
and cottage cheese. I don't know if my eyes might yet be capable of taking in the birds tumbling down from the sky, the
oranges flying in clouds, the women suckling insects. Shall I
go to the market? Will I bump into the seller of shawls, scarves,
and rebozos? Will he raise above us in the air his tent of fabrics, will he be able to keep it aloft when he wishes to speak to
me in private? Will I recognize his accent, will I know where
he comes from, whether it's from Mexico, and, if so, whether
it's from the north or south? Will the man who hauls merchandise still be anchoring around his waist the stuff the woman gives
him to carry, so that he can keep his hands free? Will he trot
along after her, the cans clattering, the plastic bags squeaking,
stepping along among the gleaming price tags, boots, packages?
Or will the market in Agustini still be selling cooking ingredi-

ents unprocessed the way Nature bestows them? The mountains of kidney beans, garbanzos, and rice—do they still await their purchasers, glistening on the ground? How old, I wonder, is the porter now? Does a child still make paper the way a child back then did? Does he still go without shoes? Does my grandmother remain asleep on the patio, stretched out on her shawl and floating? How fat has Dulce gotten by now after decades of guzzling the cakes that Lucifer makes? Do old women continue to pull out their rocking chairs to the street fronts to watch the death of the day? Are those same men still shut in the bakery? Is there even a bakery nowadays or one that actually bakes its own bread? Will the milkman come down the street, hawking his milk, banging on an empty can to alert housewives? Who still comes and goes from my house? The honey seller, the man who offers crabs, smoked lizard, and lottery tickets, along with fresh nuts and persimmon? Who is Lucifer grinding coffee for these days? Is the house still the same? Or have they shifted something out of my mother's room? Does her water jug still look out from her balcony? Old Luz's room that Dulce and Lucifer have now, does it still stink of pee? Won't Dulce be sleeping in my room now? I wonder who plays with my dolls? Or do they still await my return, on the shelf where I left them, carefully organized, well dressed, sighing for the little girl I ceased to be before I deserted them? Does Grandma still hang a bunch of bananas at the door of the kitchen so they can ripen in the shade? Do they still dry coffee and cocoa pods on the terrace that overlooks the river? Or lock the door of the living room? Does anyone ever go in there? Do the bells still shift lazily back and forth, without their clappers ever sounding? Who are the nuns getting breakfast for on Sundays? Is Grandma still invited? Will they invite me to share their delicacies if I return? Do I have the courage to return? There's no